When Tomorrow Comes

Elizabeth Manning-Ives

Published by Woodlark Publishing
Copyright © Elizabeth Manning-Ives
ISBN-13: 9780993349140
ISBN-10: 0993349140

Acknowledgements

Grateful Thanks to:

Arthur Hyde for allowing me to use his painting for the cover of this book.

Lorraine Bennett for all her hard work and assistance in preparing this book for publication.

Catherine Quinlan for encouraging me to believe in myself.

Pam Finch for her help in sourcing and providing the props which have helped to me promote this book.

Suzan Collins for all her help, support and encouragement throughout the writing and production of this book, as well as the Get Writing workshops which got me started.

Richard and Gina at the Coconut Loft in Lowestoft for their welcome, and for providing excellent cake.

Cover creation: Jen Moon

Prologue

One foggy November morning in central London in the year 1930, a young woman by the name of Amelia Woodley is lying exhausted but content on her bed. Her devoted husband Robert is sitting in an armchair beside the bed cradling their newborn twin daughters. The love he has for both his wife and the two tiny bundles he so carefully cradles is palpable. His grey-green eyes twinkle with tears and his gentle moustache-adorned mouth smiles wistfully. This delightful tableau is one of true love and contentment.

Robert and Amelia own a small clothing shop, and until now have run it themselves. But, when Amelia discovered she was pregnant, they decided very quickly that they would have to employ an assistant to help Robert with the day-to-day running of the business. Robert and Amelia have owned the shop for five years, prior to this it had been owned by Amelia's parents. It was indeed this couple who started the business when they first married, just before the turn of the century. When they retired, Robert and Amelia were delighted to take over the ownership and management; after all, this provided them, not only with financial security but also a home. The flat above the little shop was not large, but it was comfortable, and more importantly, it was theirs!

Elizabeth and Eva spend their first eight years of life being loved and protected by the most devoted parents any child could ever wish for. They are blissfully unaware of the very real and imposing danger that is about to so radically influence and change their lives forever.

It is a cold black winter night as they trudge along the road away from school. Home is still a long way off. The howling wind is biting at their faces, their hands and feet are numb. They ache all over but know they must keep going, if they arrive late their parents become anxious, and on top of the heaviness which has come over them recently, the girls are desperate not to add to their worry. This change has been more evident in Robert, but it is also showing in the sweet heart-shaped face of Amelia. When either girl asks what is wrong, both parents force a smile insisting that everything will be alright and that there is nothing to worry about. Despite their tender years, the girls have been convinced for a few days now that they are keeping something from them, trying to protect them, so are more determined than ever to please them, and arrive home on time.

Then up ahead is an enormous flash

followed by an explosion that resounds like thunder. Eva and Elizabeth stop gripped by fear. Almost immediately from behind them come the clanging bells of the fire engines, ambulances and a swarm of police, both on bicycles and on foot rushing along the road. The girls stand aside, watching them pass, and decide to move on at a quicker pace now desperate to get home.

Gradually the sky starts to get lighter and the smell of smoke gets stronger. As they turn the final corner into their street, the large leafless oak tree stands hauntingly silhouetted against the flames at the far end of their road. Fear again seizes them as they begin running towards the little shop and their home, only to be stopped halfway down by a police officer.

'You can't go any further girls everyone has been evacuated to the church hall, which number do you live at?'

Through their tears the girls reply.

'Number 34 sir, please are our mother and father alright?'

The officer calls to a colleague further down the road.

'Hey Pat are number 34 out?'

'Yes but they were worried about leaving without their daughters.'

By now the flames are leaping above the rooftops of the houses and the thick black smoke makes it difficult to breathe. The officer, now having to shout to be heard over the roar of the flames, directs the girls to the hall.

As they begin running towards safety, two figures come out of the hall. They realise that their parents have come to find them, the girls collapse into the arms of their parents sobbing with relief. They are reunited and safe, at least for the time being.

The following morning the true impact of the previous night's devastation is all too evident. Robert, Amelia, Elizabeth and Eva stand in stunned silence in front of a pile of rubble. All that the two girls have ever known has been destroyed, nothing is left. The only clothes they own are the ones they stand up in. Shivering, bemused and frightened they look to their parents for some comfort and reassurance, but despite each being wrapped in the embrace of one of their parents, what they see in both parent's faces, can only be described as a look of utter desperation and abandonment.

The stunned silence is only broken by the arrival and voice of Amelia's father James.

'The business is not important; you are all still alive and now is the best opportunity for you to move in with Elsie and myself. We are not that far from the girl's school and being away from the city centre the air is fresher for the girls to breath.'

Lowering his voice and turning away from the girls, James continues.

'It will also be easier for us to support Amelia and the girls when your time comes Robert.'

No further words are spoken, but Robert nods knowingly with a look of fear and resignation which spreads rapidly across his face. Amelia's usual rosy expression has turned to one of pallor and heartache. With shoulders slumped and feet dragging heavily, the family leave their once thriving business and happy home for the last time.

The girls will tell their own story...

Part 1

We were not quite nine years old when the war started. We didn't really understand what war meant or what was happening. We knew that father was away flying a plane, and that our mother was frightened all the time, although she tried not to let us see her fear. Both Eva and I kept trying to make her feel better and cheer her up, but her worry and thoughts were always clearly visible in her expression. For nearly a year the three of us have been together and we liked to think that our presence has helped our mother cope since father went away. But today our world is to be torn apart.

We are now nearly ten and the bombing has been going on for a few weeks, and now parents are being told to send their children away from the city to the safety of the countryside. So, early one morning, our mother takes us to the train station. Along with many of our friends, we are being ushered onto the waiting train. We are leaving everything we know and everyone who loves us. Even though she tries to smile, both of us can see the tears in mother's eyes just waiting to escape when we are out of her view.

'Oh mother, why do we have to go?'
Her reply is as kind as she always is, although it sounds almost hollow.

'To keep you safe my darlings.'

'But we feel safe with you, please don't make us go.'
She makes no reply but hugs and kisses us both as we are ushered firmly onto the train.

As the journey begins we are both heart-broken and terrified. At the same time, the tears we have been holding back now fall freely from our eyes. Looking out of the window, we can see the scene changing, becoming less and less familiar. Trees replace buildings, and fields and rivers replace roads. It is like another world to us, one that we will have to get to know whether we want to or not. The soft blue sunlit sky of the winter morning has become slate grey, dull with clouds gathering fast. Our small amount of luggage which is made up of two tiny, battered, brown suitcases, a paper bag each and our gasmasks, looks as abandoned as we are both feeling, and the food in the brown paper bags is not even for us, but for the strangers who are to take us into their home. Our mother has told us that whatever happens we must stay together, so not to let anyone separate us. Our gas masks hang in their boxes round our necks and labels with our names on them have been tied to our coats. When mother had hugged and kissed us goodbye that morning we had not wanted her to ever let go, and we are already really missing the security of home. This is the first time in our lives we have been completely alone. Again we start to cry.

With the long train journey finally over, it is surprisingly nice to feel fresh air again. Although we are no longer crying, both of us feel numb and uncertain about what will happen next. The stark imposing image of the church lit up against the ever darkening sky and misty horizon is our first view of the village where we are to stay. It makes a lasting impression on us as we are only nine years old and are clinging to each other for comfort. We walk down a road, and in spite of the dark night the little white fences are still clearly visible. Horses and carts, not cars are the main danger in this small, strange place. The buildings are different too, with their roofs made of straw, and gardens with shrubs and other plants everywhere. By the time we reach the church hall our legs are aching, and the gloom inside the building reflects the stark image that first greeted us. The whole place feels friendless and cold, adding to our misery.

We are all made to stand with our backs against the wall so that we can be seen. A parade for the people who we are to be living with. One by one children are taken by strangers; my friends have already gone before a couple who have their own little girl finally agree to take us with them. They really only wanted one of us, but we refuse to be separated, so reluctantly they take us both. We leave with them, hoping that their little girl will become our friend, but when her father speaks to his wife these hopes fade rapidly.

'Well, at least we will get paid for taking them in.'

We soon realise that this family don't really want us at all. Looking at Eva, I can see that we are feeling exactly the same; our mouths are dry and our stomachs so tight they feel knotted. We know that we are not going to sleep tonight. Their little girl, whose name is Ann does not even speak; she just looks at us as if we are intruding, then turns away. When we reach the house our bags of food are snatched away without a word. Then it is Ann's mother who speaks, but her tone is cold and harsh.

'You two girls, follow me. Bring your belongings and be quick about it!'

We are led up two flights of stairs to a large draughty room with only a bed and two wooden stools in it, that they called the attic. We don't belong here, we are not welcome,

13

we are obviously going to be kept out of the way, and not included in the family anymore than necessary.

This first night away from home is feeling very strange, we have been so used to the sound of bombs falling, and air raid sirens blaring, the silence of the countryside is empty and eerie. Our large room is dark and scary; we huddle together for comfort but are both shaking and still sniffing loudly. As we lay here shivering under the rough, scratchy blankets, unable to sleep, the fear which has been building in us since our arrival earlier today is stopping us from doing so. We are becoming aware of noises all around us and throughout the house. At first it is just the odd creak of a floor board or what sounds like twigs scrapping the window, but they are soon joined by the howling of the wind and the thud of the shutters on the wall outside our window. We pull the covers tighter around our ears trying to muffle the myriad of noises, but they just seem to be getting louder and louder. We know that our presence here is not really wanted so dare not leave our room for fear of being beaten. Yet as time goes on we are too frightened to stay.

Eventually, we decide that we would be better off trying to get back home to mother, the bombs are terrifying it is true, but at least our mother loves us and we know what all the noises are. We dress quickly and quietly, although without a light this is quite a struggle. When we know for certain that everyone else is in bed, we slowly turn the handle of the attic door and open it trying not to let it creak. But, we both know from living with our grandparents in their old house for the last few months since the explosion, just before our father left to join the RAF that all doors of a certain age creak. We make it out into the corridor without much of a creak and begin to make our way along it towards the narrow steep staircase, and then along a much grander hallway towards the large wide staircase. On the landing halfway down, the suits of armour stand threateningly, as though poised for action. A shiver chases through us both! We begin to descend the stairs, and then we hear it. Distant and echoing to begin with, but with each step we take down the stairs; it becomes louder and more intense.

'Lizzie, what is that noise?'

'I don't know Eva. I don't like either, but if we want to get back to our own dear mother, we must leave here tonight. Come on, at least we are together.'

We continue with greater caution than before, but with even more determination.

We reach the landing with the armour on it and freeze, gripped with terror we are unable to go on or go back. A cold rush of air passes

15

by us at great speed, and the noise begins to fade.

'Did you see something Eva?'

'I don't know, do you think the noise and the cold air are linked Lizzie?'

'They must be, what is this place we have been sent too Eva?'

'What is going on here?'

We stop talking for fear of being heard, but one thing we are certain of is that we are not safe if we stay. So, quickening our pace we begin once again to descend the stairs, but before we can even take three steps another noise begins to build and before we know what is happening we are running down the remaining stairs. But, Eva reaches the bottom in a heap as she misses her footing and tumbles down the last few. I help her up quickly, and we head straight for the huge front door, only to discover that our escape has been denied. The great door is bolted top and bottom and although we can reach the one at the bottom and turn the large key in the lock, the top bolt is well out of our reach. With tears stinging our eyes we decide we have no choice, but to go back to our room in the attic and wait until morning, but with the knowledge that we are not staying here whatever happens!

After climbing back into the huge old bed we are sharing, even more awake than before, the black cloak of night is almost a comfort. As we stare into its all-consuming endlessness, despite our terror we eventually fall asleep however, and when we awake next morning, instead of noisy traffic, all we can hear are birds singing, and running water which appears to be coming from the bottom of the garden.

Although it is November, and in spite of the horrible noises of last night, the day starts fine and bright if a little chilly. So, after breakfast we decide to go out into the garden. We want to slip out unnoticed so that we can try and find our way back to London. But Ann takes great pleasure in spoiling our plans immediately by telling her parents our intentions. How did she know what we were planning to do? Had she been spying on us last night and overheard our whispered conversation? However she found out we are the ones suffering now! As punishment for being so ungrateful, they insist that we wash and dry all the breakfast things, before telling us that we are to attend the little village school every morning. This fills us with dread, but as we walk through the gate a friendly young boy called Billy greets us with more warmth than we could have imagined. Could this be our one ray of light in the horror we find ourselves in? Unfortunately we are only able to be in school until lunchtime because there are too many children for us all to be there all day, so time spent with our friends from London is short, but also helps to shine a light into the darkness which surrounds us. The older children go in the afternoon.

We are in the same class as Ann, but she is still refusing to talk to us, and she seems to be keeping all the other children away from us whether they are her friends or not. Eva and I cannot help feeling as though she hates and resents us, but we don't know why. Is it because we are from London? We feel more lonely and miserable than ever.

We leave school at lunchtime fully intending to seek out the railway station and head back to London, but Billy is so eager to show us the farm where he lives and the woods nearby. As he has been so friendly towards us we don't want him to be hurt, so we decide to go with him. We are certainly in no hurry to return to the house where we are not wanted. Unfortunately Ann catches us at the gate.

'Where are you going with Billy then? You will be in big trouble when you do get back, his family are heathens. If you mix with them you will be punished, I'll tell father and then you'll be for it.'

Eva and I are so surprised, not only by the level of spite she has in her voice, but more simply because this is the first time she has said anything to us since we arrived yesterday. Before we can recover enough to answer her, both she and her friends have started walking away giggling and whispering. It is Billy who speaks next.

'Maybe you'd better not come, if you're staying with them that is.'

'But why not? Don't you want us to come with you now? Please say you don't hate us too.'

'Hey now, of course I still want you to come, and I don't hate no-one. It's just that...'

'Just what Billy?'

'Well, I shouldn't really talk about folks if they're not here to defend themselves, but I feel sorry for Ann, she always looks so sad and lonely. Those girls she's with aren't really friends; they only stay with her because her pa owns the big house. Her poor ma is the person I feel most sorry for, never being allowed to go nowhere if he's not with her. My pa reckons he rules his house with a rod of iron.'

In spite of the fear we are both feeling, which is now increasing rapidly, we cannot help giggling at Billy's accent.

'Hey, what's so funny? What are you laughing at?'

'Please Billy, don't think us cruel or impolite, but we have never heard an accent like yours before.'

'Ah, I thought as much, you London lot sound strange to us too you know. You think you're speaking properly, but when you live on a farm like we do, there is no need for airs and graces. So, are you coming with me or not?'

Eva looks at me and I look at her, then without much of a pause, we smile and agree to go with Billy.

'My ma will be really made up that you decided to come, she has never met no-one from London before.'

We reach the little straw-roofed farmhouse faster than we could have hoped, but even though Billy charges straight in through the back door, we hover in the doorway until formerly invited to enter.

'Billy, is that you crashing in like a herd of cattle?'

'Aye ma, and my new friends, come all the way from London they have.'

'Well, where are your manners lad, bring them in, don't leave them standing in the doorway. Come in my dears you're most welcome here, no need to be shy with us. My, my, whatever is the matter? You both look scared out of your wits.'

'They're staying at the big house ma, with Ann and her folks.'

Billy's mother says no more, but glances

gravely towards Billy us she ushers us into the warmth of the well-lit kitchen.

The warm friendliness of this little farm is so welcome after the cold austerity of our lodgings that the afternoon is over far too quickly.

'I wanted to show them the woods ma, but you lot have kept them talking so long that it is too dark now.'

'Oh stop your moaning Billy; the woods are no place for two young girls in the middle of winter anyway.'

'Then, looking concerned and even more grave than before she continues.

'Right our Billy, you make sure these little lasses get back to their lodgings safely, do you hear me?'

'Yes ma, but I wish I didn't have to take them back to that place.'

'Hush Billy, do as you are told and don't you go telling them any of your silly rumours.'

We leave the happiness and welcome of the farm, and begin the long cold, bleak walk back to the place we dread more than anywhere else. The rather grand size and look of the place does not even begin to reflect the horror we feel as we approach it.

'Are you going to be alright from here? Only I daren't come no closer.'

Holding firmly to each other's hands we nod

and smile at Billy, watching him flee from view before we walk the last few yards towards this place of terror. Everything in us is telling us to go the other way, to try and find the station, but as we stand quaking at the end of the path the huge front door opens. The silhouetted figure standing in the doorway is the unmistakable figure of Ann's father.

'You two! Get in here now!'
The sharpness in his tone and booming nature of his voice only causes us to become even more rigid and unable to move.

'Don't make me come out there and get you, or you will regret it even more. Your supper is already spoiled. If I had my way you would have no supper, but I will not be accused of starving anyone in my care, even you. Move it!'
Clutching each other's hands even more tightly we start running, although not fast enough to avoid a sharp pain across both our backs when he swipes us with his leather belt as we pass. This causes us to stumble, but we do not fall, and dare not show our pain. Beatings are so unfamiliar to us, but our fear is that this is only the first of many.

'While you are guests in my house you will abide by my rules. Cavorting with heathens indeed! From tomorrow you will return home at lunchtime with Ann and have

22

nothing more to do with Billy Elder. I will ensure you learn the error of your ways. Go to the attic this instant, and if I see you down here again tonight you will feel my strap more than once!'

It is with a sense of relief that we escape to the attic tonight, and although our supper is already waiting for us up there we cannot eat anything now. Only now do we feel safe to cry, but we still do not know why we were hit, what a heathen is or what we have done wrong? But, one thing we are determined about is that even if we are beaten for it, Billy and his family are the only people to show us any friendship or kindness since our arrival here, so we will not be stopped from seeing him and spending time with him.

As we climb into bed tonight, memories of the terror we felt and experienced last night are vivid in our minds. But, knowing that the front door will be bolted, escape is not an option. We huddle together quickly, pulling the covers tightly around us, not only against the chill of winter as it creeps into the draughty attic, but more to give each other comfort and much needed courage.

Sleep remains a long way off and our backs are still stinging from being hit with the belt, but the velvet cloak of night provides security and even a little comfort. The noises from our first night seem less real and intimidating to us now, and cannot be heard tonight. In fact, it is so quiet that we are almost longing to hear the twigs scrapping against the window or the shutters thudding against the wall, but the wind is not so strong tonight, so there is very little movement outside. However, after a while our eyes are beginning to feel heavy, and for the first time since we arrived, sleep feels as though it may come to us. But, this peace does not last long. Below us in the main part of the house a door slams, and Ann's father's unmistakeable voice can be heard shouting once again.

Now, wide awake once more, we lay here straining to hear what he is yelling, and who his temper is aimed at. But, although he is shouting, being so far above means that individual words are hard to make out, but it is not long before the door slams again and footsteps can be heard climbing the main staircase. Trembling, we wait for our door to open, but it is a relief when the footsteps stay on the floor below. Then, another sound, this time it is the sound of somebody crying, but it is not a child-like cry, it sounds more like the type of crying which mother often did since father went to war.

Things are definitely not happy or loving in this place. After a few more minutes, heavier footsteps can be heard coming up the stairs below us, but again they do not come up to the attic. The strangest thing is though, they do not sound as if they go in the same direction as the first ones we heard. We have never heard shouting and yelling like that which we have heard tonight before. Our parents never argue, all we have ever known is love.

***

We are missing home more and more, we got a letter from our mother on our birthday but they appeared not even to notice. Now Christmas is coming and many of our friends are going home, but our mother wants us to stay here. Does she not want us anymore? We know things in London are bad and that she says she doesn't want us to get hurt, but we really don't know whether to believe her or not. We haven't told her how bad things are here, she will only worry and she is worried enough about father. Every night we pray for things to get better, and for Christmas to be happy and fun. But waking up each morning it is obvious nothing has, or is even likely to change before then.

After another uncertain and restless night, we have woken to find a very different looking world this morning, and an even colder feel to our already chilly attic.

'Elizabeth, come quickly, look!'

Grabbing my very thin, but essential dressing gown I reluctantly stumble out of bed and across the floor to peer out of the one tiny window.

'What is it Eva? It is even colder up here this morning.'

'Yes, it is and if you look outside you will discover what has caused such a feel.'
We are both now standing, gazing out onto a thick white blanket of snow which is stretching its sparkling icy fingers as far as we can see in all directions.

'Come on, let's get dressed quickly and slip out no-one here will miss us. Maybe we can find the station and go back to London!'
A new excitement and real sense of hope is beginning to build in both of us, but this too is snatched away from our grasp almost before it begins.

'Wait Eva, listen! Someone is crying again, only this time it sounds more like Ann.'

'What do you think is going on here Elizabeth?'

'I don't know, but whatever it is, I fear our presence here is only making things worse.'

'Maybe we can help, we should at least try. You know that mother has always told us to help where we can hasn't she?'

'I know Eva, but she has also told us not to involve ourselves in things which do not concern us!'

We stand shivering for several minutes just

staring at each other, but in my heart I know that Eva is right. We should at least check to see if Ann is alright, even if she has made our lives miserable since we got here. Perhaps Billy was right all along; maybe she is sad and lonely. None of this is her fault, her father John is obviously not a nice man, and we are both certain that her mother Agnes was crying last night. We dress quickly, putting on the warmest clothes we have, although knowing they will prove of little defence in these conditions, and begin our journey down the steep narrow staircase from the attic. Ann's crying gets louder as we approach the door to her room, but before we can knock on it, John's voice booms at his wife from inside another room, followed by footsteps moving rapidly towards the door next to Ann's. We change direction immediately, and feeling trapped, begin making our way back towards our attic. Before we reach the bottom of our staircase however, a door opens and a trembling voice urges us to enter the room from which it comes. Turning round we see Ann trembling, and with a look of terror in her eyes which are already red from much crying.

'Whatever is the matter Ann? What has happened?'

'Shh! You better get in here quick, or father will start again.'

'Start what?'

'Not out here!'

Feeling caught between two different snares we are unable to move for what feels like several minutes, but in reality cannot be more than a few seconds because no sooner are we in Ann's room with the door closed, John can be heard leaving the room next door in what can only be described as a fit of utter rage.

'Ann are you alright? We heard you crying and wanted to help you if we can. We know you don't really want us here, but we didn't have a choice. We have been sent here to escape the constant bombing in London.'

`I don't mean to be so unkind, it is just that father told me that you wouldn't want to be friends with me, and that if I was too friendly you would want to stay here and not go home. He told me that children from London were all trouble makers and thieves, and that if you were nice to me, I wasn't to trust you because you would steal all my things. I am so sorry that you are having to stay with us, not because I don't want you here, but because father can be really mean and I worry that you will think we are all like that.'

'Oh Ann, you must get so lonely and frightened here all alone, we have only ever wanted to be your friend. We just thought you resented and hated us, so when Billy wanted us to be his friend we said yes because we miss home and mother so much. We just want to feel as if we belong for as long as we are here.'

'I was jealous when I saw you with him, which is why I told you not to go with him, I only told father because he threatened to beat me if I didn't, and then when you got home he beat you instead. That is why mother was so upset last night; they had a row about it.'

'But Ann, Billy told us that he feels sorry for you, we are sure he will be your friend too.'

'I only wish that could happen. Father would never allow it.'

'But why not? What is so bad about him and his family, they are so kind and welcoming?'

For a while the three of us just stand looking at each other, waiting to for someone to speak, but no-one seems to know what to say. Eventually we hear the front door being unlocked and unbolted, as someone goes outside banging the door hard behind them. We continue to listen as the footsteps crunching through the snow fade as the person moves further into the distance.

'That will be father; he has gone for one of his walks. He does that when he is in a temper.'

'Please Ann; tell us why your father hates Billy's family so much?'

'Well, I don't know very much, but I will tell you what I do know if you promise never to tell father or mother that you know.'
We both agree, and eventually take a seat on Ann's bed ready to listen to all that she can tell with great interest.

'All I know is that Billy's mother is my father's younger sister, and that father didn't want to take over the family farm, spending the rest of his life stuck in one place doing the type of work he considers to be menial and beneath him. He left home at eighteen, telling his parents that he hated being poor so he was going to better himself and become rich.

He has certainly been able to make a lot of money, and by the time he married mother, he had turned his back completely on his family. This has been very hard for my mother to understand or accept, because family is and always has been very important to her. So for a long while she tried to continue to maintain contact with her family, and, without his knowledge have some contact with his as well. But, eventually he became so controlling and suspicious that even contact with her own family is no longer possible. She isn't even allowed to see her own parents now! I have therefore, never known any of my grandparents, and if I ever ask about them father just yells and frightens me so much that I have to hide up. I often hear my poor mother crying and long to be able to help her feel better, but am too frightened to go to her in case father catches me.

'Do his parents still live at the farm Ann?'

'No, not anymore. Unfortunately they both died, only days apart, two years ago. He didn't even go to their funerals because they were not held at the big church. His sister still wants to be his friend, even after all the awful treatment and years of isolation she has suffered, but because they go to chapel, instead of the church we go to, father does not want anything to do with them, in fact he won't even acknowledge their existence.'

'But surely your father used to go to the chapel as a child didn't he?'

Before Ann can even begin to answer this question, the front door opens and, once again her father's voice can be heard in the hallway at the bottom of the stairs, before entering one of the rooms below us.

'Well, I've never known that before! The school is closed because of the weather; I suppose that means those two little trouble-makers will be here all day. Well they are not going to waste their time; they can help around the house while they are here and use

31

their time in a productive way. Agnes, you are to watch that pair closely at all times, they cannot be trusted. Cavorting with heathens indeed, they will not make that mistake again.'

'John, they are only children, it cannot be easy for them being so far from home, and Billy was only being friendly. Goodness knows they haven't received much in the way of friendship since they arrived; you even set our own daughter against them! Please let me talk to them and try to find out something about them and their family. We do not expect our own daughter to undertake household chores; I will not allow you to turn our guests into servants!'

'You are not to undermine my authority in my house; you should know that by now! I know quite enough, I summed those two up as soon as I saw them! You only have to look at them to know they are not to be trusted. They are to be kept away from Ann as much as possible; I will not have our daughter corrupted by children like that! You are too gullible and soft-hearted for your own good, I will take charge of those two today. They'll not get into mischief under my roof.'

A door downstairs slams shut, and his footsteps can be heard pounding up the stairs at great speed.

'Now we're in trouble, how are we

going to get back to our room without being caught?'

Looking at Ann's face, it is obvious that she is as terrified as we are. But, to our relief, after a short pause, his footsteps head away from Ann's room following the same direction they travelled in last night.

'Quick, now is your chance, he is in Tom's room, he'll be in there for at least twenty minutes.'

'Who's Tom?'

'Not now, there's no time, I'll explain later when it is safe, now go!'

Hearing the urgency and panic in Ann's voice, we make our escape quickly to the peace of the attic. However, it is with fear that we wait for the inevitable footsteps, or more likely, a commanding voice from the bottom of our narrow stairs issuing us with our orders for the day. The lack of heat in this attic and our sense of impending doom for what the rest of the day will bring for us causes both of us to start shivering. So much seems to have changed this morning, and yet Ann's father still seems to hate us and resent our presence here.

We have so many unanswered questions now, but the one that is intriguing us most of all is, who is Tom? Until this morning both Eva and I had assumed that Ann was an only child. Has she got a brother? Is he kept hidden in that room? Does he even really exist? We do not have long to ponder these questions however, before the booming voice we learned to fear in less than a week of being here, yells at us from the bottom of the attic stairs.

'You two, get down here immediately! You may not be going to school today, but you will certainly learn some valuable lessons in obedience, and make yourselves useful while you are here!'
We are already halfway down the stairs before he has finished shouting.

'Well, at least you heeded my warning. Now, to the kitchen and to work!'
The fact that we have not had any breakfast this morning makes no difference, and in spite of the hunger we both feel, having not eaten last night either, we both know that we are better off not to say anything. At least this room is warm, and whatever we are going to have to do , it is bound to better than freezing to death in the attic, where the frost is on the inside of the windows as well as the outside, and the icy wind rattles it in its frame.
Our first job is to wash, dry, and put away all the breakfast things, which we do as quickly and carefully as we can, but neither of us is very tall, so water gets splashed onto the floor, and we have to use a stool to reach the cupboards. Nothing gets broken, but the

34

water on the floor is seen before we can clean it up, so as punishment for making a mess we are made to scrub the whole floor. This takes a really long time, and our hands are red and sore well before we finish the job. By now we both feel like crying, but are determined to hold back any tears while we are being so closely watched. With the floor scrubbed and dried, both Eva and myself are feeling so tired we begin to long to be back in the attic, however cold and draughty it is. But, soon any hope of this becoming reality is cruelly dashed as our next task is given to us.

'Right, now you can begin preparing the vegetables for lunch. Eva, you can peel and chop the potatoes and Elizabeth, you can do the carrots. The knives are sharp so be careful! When you have finished that, you can take yourselves back up to the attic, perhaps then, a letter to your mother would be a good idea.'

While at the house we spend most of our time in the attic room, and today is no exception. We even eat all our meals up there. We are still feeling unwanted, although this morning has given us a glimmer of hope with Ann at least. When we are downstairs we are usually blamed for everything that goes wrong, especially by Ann's father. Her mother seems to be softening towards us, and is starting to try to make things better for us when her husband is not around, but the more time that passes, the more certain we become that she is scared of him too.

We try our hardest with the preparation of the potatoes and carrots, but unfortunately with very little success. Eventually with a great deal of irritation, Ann's father snatches the knives out of hands and firmly dismisses us to the attic with strict instructions to write our letters home. As we are climbing the main staircase, once again we can hear crying coming from one of the rooms. However, it soon becomes clear that it is not coming from Ann's room, and it does not sound as if it is coming from her mother's room either. We stand and listen, but dare not move towards the sound for fear of being caught, but it appears to be coming from the direction of Tom's room.

We are still standing, listening, when a door opens behind us. Terrified, we dare not even turn round, instead, we run towards the narrow staircase and up it as quickly as we can, closing the door firmly behind us. We both collapse, panting on to the large hard bed that we share.

'That was too close, who do you think saw us standing there Elizabeth?'

'I don't know, but we had better stay up here and not make any noise Eva, at least for a little while?

'I suppose you're right, I just wish it wasn't so cold.'

After a few minutes, and no obvious sign of being pursued, we are both starting to feel a little calmer, so begin writing our letters home as instructed, fearing greatly what will befall us if we don't.

However, we have not been back up in the attic for long, when we hear footsteps climbing the same narrow stairs that we had climbed a few minutes earlier and approach the door to our room. Frozen with fear and unable to move, we sit waiting for our door to open. But something is different; the footsteps are too light to belong to Ann's father, but too heavy to be Ann's. The footsteps stop, and there is a long pause before a gentle tap on our door breaks the tense silence.

'Girls, can I come in please? I need to talk to you while John is out of the house. The truth will come out eventually, and I would rather you here it from me.'

It is quite a surprise to hear the voice of Ann's mother outside the door. She has barely spoken to us since the day we arrived, and then she appeared as cold and unloving as her husband.

'Of course you can come in, we are living in your house so you should not need to ask us, we are just writing our letters home.'

There is another short pause before the door actually opens and Ann's mother enters.

We can already sense that this meeting with her is going to be very different from the day of our arrival. Her expression is so much softer, although full of melancholy and her voice is not nearly so harsh and cold, in fact it has a strange but almost musical quality about it.

'I would never enter a guest's room without knocking first, and for as long as you remain here you are my guests. You girls really are good to write home as often as you do, each letter must bring such comfort to your poor dear mother. She must miss you both terribly, especially with your father away and the future of your whole dear little family so uncertain.'

For the first time since leaving London, the reality of the situation is becoming all too clear to us. We have always known that father's absence is the cause of mother's constant fear, but it is only now that the true horror of it all and what could happen is finally beginning to sink in.

'Do you really think that our father could never come home?'

Tears are stinging my eyes intensely, but I dare not let them escape. However, when I finally dare to glance up at Eva and then at

Ann's mother, I realise that I am not alone in feeling this sense of despair and hopelessness which now seems to be filling the already chilly attic with an even more intensely cold atmosphere.

'Oh my dears, I did not mean that, you must remain hopeful and pray continually for your father's safe return. I was referring more to the uncertainty surrounding our dear country, and how much of it will remain untouched by this horrible war. We will all have a great deal of rebuilding to do when it is over, I doubt whether any of our lives will ever be the same again.'

If this is supposed to comfort us, it fails miserably. The only thing it succeeds in doing is making the enforced separation from our mother and father even harder to bear. It is also clear by looking at Agnes's face that she doesn't believe what she is saying anymore than Eva or I do, nevertheless we say nothing and allow her to continue.

'I have come to see you now so that I can try and explain a few things to you. Please let me start by apologising for the somewhat hostile reception you received on your arrival here. Both John and I were concerned about taking unknown children into our home, and the effect that your presence here would have on Ann. We also knew it was our duty to help in any way we could, so eventually we agreed. My husband is not an easy man, and until now I have not had the courage to go against him in anything, but this is changing, although, my new found confidence has bought its own challenges and more than a little conflict between us. In spite of John's reluctance and harsh insistence that I obey his every word, I am beginning to see the need for wider family and friendships. Family has always been of great value and importance to me, this war and your presence here has made me realise the need to stand up for these things. I am so glad that you and Ann are finally able to begin building a friendship, she is so isolated here alone, and I know now that we were quite wrong to try and keep her away from you. Unfortunately John has always found it extremely difficult to accept anyone new after his relationship with his own family broke down so dramatically. I fear he still hasn't forgiven himself for not making amends with his parents before they died. It is my belief that it is for this reason he could not face going to their funerals. This means he is very strict, and at times his cruel discipline makes life very hard for Ann and me, so I am asking you to please be patient with him. I hope and pray that in time he too will come to see your presence here as a positive thing for our daughter as I have. I also hope you will, in time be able to forgive us all for the treatment you have received here since you arrived. I can only imagine how terrified and homesick you both were, and still are I imagine, but from now on Ann and I will try to make your stay with us more like home. This, we can only do without John's knowledge at the moment for the reasons I have already explained, but please believe me when I say he will not beat you again, or work you as he did this morning. He knows that I am not in favour of such treatment, and I have told him that I will not tolerate any more of it.

The other reason for me coming to you now is much more personal and painful for me to explain, but I am telling you because it may go some way towards helping you understand John's very hard and almost military attitude. I understand from talking to Ann this morning, that she happened to mention Tom, and that you have heard and seen things coming from and near the locked room at the end of the corridor opposite Ann's room. What I am about to tell you may seem unkind or strange, but please believe me when I tell you that, for your own safety and protection as well as Tom's, you must not attempt to enter that room, or ask any questions of anyone other than me. If I could, I would have you down in a room in the main house with us, but you are so much safer up here.'

Our sense of fear is growing rapidly now, and must show more than we realise because suddenly, for the first time since we got here, Agnes puts an arm around each of us and draws us towards her. This unexpected sign of affection should be welcome and help ease our minds; instead, it only makes us feel more fearful and even a little uncomfortable. However, something in both of us prevents Eva or me from pulling away, and for me at least, I get the sense that Agnes needs to feel this closeness for herself as well as trying to reassure us. Taking a deep breath and a long pause Ann's mother continues, only now her voice is even more gentle and sounds almost shaky.

'I am sure your question to Ann this morning regarding Tom's identity must still be eating away at your curiosity. I know that if I were in your position it would be like that for me, so I will start the story there. How much did Ann tell you about her father's family this morning?'
Eva and I sit either side of Ann's mother, still wrapped in the rather awkward embrace and glance at each other anxiously. Is this a trap? Is she trying to trip us up or get us in to trouble for talking to her daughter? Are we going to get Ann into trouble if we tell her mother what she shared with us?

'Come now girls, please do not be so anxious, neither you nor Ann will be in any trouble. Depending on how much you already know she may well have made this easier for me.'

'Well ma'am, we know that Billy's mother is your husband's sister, and that he never wanted to take over the farm. Ann also said that the reason he refused to even talk to his family, is because they don't attend the same church as you, but we don't know anymore.'

'Well then, at least I know where to start, although I am sure you will be shocked by much of what you learn. My husband's decision not to acknowledge his sister and her family goes much deeper than them attending chapel instead of church, in fact it has very little to do with that at all. But, before I explain this part of the story, I must first explain about Tom.

Billy's mother is indeed my husband's younger sister, but John is not the eldest child. Tom is the older brother to both of them. After Tom was born his mother was very ill for a long while, and was strongly advised not to have any other children as her health and body would be unable to cope with the trauma of it. For a young newly married woman those words were the hardest of all to hear. However, for ten long years after Tom's birth, she followed that advice. Then, her desire to have more children began to consume and overwhelm her. So, despite being warned again that a pregnancy could end her life and deprive Tom of his mother, her husband was so concerned that the anguish of not having another child would be just as bad for her health, he reluctantly agreed that they should try. It did not take long for John to appear, and thankfully this time she suffered very little and soon settled into a routine, even looking and feeling stronger than she had for years. She was so happy to have her two boys, and Tom doted on John from the very beginning. But, when John was still only eight months old their mother discovered that she was pregnant again. This was quite a shock, and although initially things went well, when Joan was born, it again nearly cost their devoted mother her life. This time she never fully recovered, and was left weak and frail. She loved her new baby girl enormously, as she continued to love her two boys, but despite her best efforts, she struggled every day to fulfil her role as a wife and mother.

Eventually, her husband was left with no choice but to employ a manager to take care of the day-to-day running of the farm, so that he could take over many of the duties at home. Tom, who was now twelve, took on some of the easier tasks on the farm, such as collecting the eggs, milking the cows and feeding all the animals. This was on top of already helping with the harvest which he had done since he was ten. Tom quite enjoyed his new responsibilities, as he felt grown up and free out in the open. The little family lived happily, in spite of their considerable challenges, for a few years.

Then, just as now, war broke out and everything changed rapidly.'

Eva and I are listening intently, and fighting back tears already. It is as though we can really feel the years of pain Ann's poor father must have been through. But we are struggling to understand why his wife should choose to share such a painful, personal story with us, two children from London, who they had been forced to have in their house. But then I begin to wonder whether perhaps she needs someone to share this burden with, and because we are still almost strangers, maybe she finds it easier to tell us than someone she knows well or cares for.

'When the first war started in 1914, Tom was fourteen years old and quite happy to continue to help on the farm. But in 1916 this changed, many of the younger farm hands who Tom had grown up with and become friends with over the years, were forced to join the army and go off to war to fight for their King and country.'

'Do you mean like our father is now?'

'Yes Eva, very much like that. Tom became restless and was desperate to join them, but, to the great relief of his parents, he was not yet old enough. He was not yet sixteen, and the official age for enlisting was eighteen. This frustrated him enormously, and although for a few months he was he was encouraged to stay by his father, when he was given greater responsibility in the tasks he was given to do around the farm, his new satisfaction was short-lived.

So, early one morning, before anyone else was awake, he packed his bag and left after writing a short letter to his parents explaining his decision and sudden absence. When this letter was discovered on the kitchen table that morning, the shock and distress proved too much for his mother and, once again she was confined to her bed. Her husband tried so hard to console her with the knowledge that he would not be accepted because he was not old enough. However, this failed to bring her any comfort, and eventually after a whole week had passed without him returning, even he had to admit they were clinging on to false hope.'

'But if he wasn't old enough, why did he not go back home?'

'Shh! Eva, we must not ask such

46

questions.'

'It is quite alright Elizabeth, Eva's question is perfectly acceptable, and one that I would want an answer too as well if I were your age. Tom did not return home because although he had lied about his age, the time he had spent working on the farm, meant that he looked old enough.

Throughout the next two years the family prayed constantly for Tom's safe return, but the war came to an end, in November, and that Christmas passed with no news. Easter also came and went without the family receiving any word from or about Tom. Then, at the end of May, when everyone had just about given up any hope of ever seeing Tom alive again, an uncertain knock at the door appeared to answer their long awaited for and heart-felt desire. At least when they first opened it and saw Tom standing there, they thought it had. But, the Tom who stood before them now was no longer the fresh-faced farm boy who had left them three years earlier, in fact he was unrecognisable. His once vibrant blue eyes seemed dark, lifeless and hollow, and although he spoke to everyone calling them all by name, it was obvious that this man standing in their presence was thin, deeply hurting and broken.'

Ann's mother pauses, swallowing hard,

breathing deeply and blinking to disguise the threatening tears that visibly glisten on her eyelashes.

'Are you alright ma'am?'

'I'm fine girls, just taking a moment, are you alright? Do you want me to stop?'
The choking sadness we are feeling causes our voices to sound croaky, but we are determined to hear the full story.

'We too are fine, please don't stop.'

'Very well then if you are sure. Tom was not home for long when things began to show, which greatly concerned his parents. They began to fear for the safety of John and little Joan. So, after only a few weeks, Tom was forced to leave the farm forever, and would never inherit it as was his birthright as the eldest son. Despite being only eight years old, John hated his parents for sending his brother away, vowing from that day that he would never take over the farm. John had always idolised his brother, and now they were being separated again.

The tragic reality of this situation was that Joan's safety had been the main concern, and it was not a lack of love for their eldest son that caused his parents to send him away, but ignorance and a lack of education. They were unable to understand that he was not dangerous, but in desperate need of understanding and love.'

Ann's mother stops talking immediately and we pull away from her embrace, as down in the main house we hear the front door open, and Ann's father re-enters calling to his wife.

'I must go now girls, but I will return and tell you the rest I promise.'
Without another word she leaves our little attic room and makes her way down the narrow stairs so fast we fear she may stumble and fall, but she reaches the floor below safely, and can soon be heard descending the main staircase, calling back to her husband.

***

Today is Sunday, and as usual we are expected to attend church. Although this is nothing unusual to us as it has been part of our lives for as long as we can remember, we never feel comfortable here. It wouldn't be so bad if we were allowed to sit with Ann, but her father still insists that we sit alone at the back. He says that we might show him up with our 'London manners'. This is both hurtful and insulting to us as we have always been complemented on our manners at home, but we dare not let our feelings show for fear of being beaten. In spite of the promise that Ann's mother made us, Ann's father seldom misses an opportunity to make our lives even more miserable. If he gets the chance, he will still try to swipe at us with a belt, or even his hand if we happen to get in his way.

Christmas is now only a week away, and far from improving, things seem to be getting worse. When Ann's father gets angry, there are times now when we are locked in our room with no food or drink. We cry ourselves to sleep regularly, and often lay awake in the total darkness, the blackouts at the windows shutting out all light. We long for the gentle moonlight and friendly twinkle of the stars that we had found comfort in at home before the war started. We often still ask ourselves if our mother sent us away because she blames us for all the things that went wrong, just like Ann's father appears to now, but deep down we know this is not true. Our only real consolation is having each other and our friendships with Billy and Ann. But any time spent with either of them is rare, and can only happen when Ann's father is not at home.

This time of year is usually so happy and filled with fun for us, but this year is so very different. A small tree stands in the corner with a few parcels underneath it for Ann, but so far nothing for us, even from our own mother. But this morning a parcel has arrived from her with ribbons in it for our hair. However, they are snatched away immediately, and given to Ann by her father despite her protesting that they belonged to us. She is firmly put in her place and told not to argue, and we are told that we are being selfish not to share them with her. We are also told that she is more deserving of them than we are, as she is better behaved. We feel abandoned and rejected all over again, and our desperation to run away back to London is growing by the day, whether it is safe or not. We are to share in the goose for dinner, but as always we eat together in our room. Instead of laughter and fun, we spend much of today sobbing. We do manage to keep our new teddies thanks to Ann's mother, these had arrived a week earlier, and because she had met the postman, she was able to take them straight up to the attic without the knowledge of her husband. They had been waiting for us when we returned from school that day. Scruffy Bear is hidden under my side of the bed, and Eloise under Eva's side; we still don't think Ann's father knows about them. We love them both dearly, but all we really want is to be back with our own mother. We need a hug and her kind, loving smile. Just a few gentle words of comfort so that we know she still cares about us. We cry more and more as the weeks go by.

Part 2

With Christmas now a few weeks behind us, and winter still holding this place in the harshest grip that people have known for several years, our life with Ann and her parents has changed very little. Ann still longs for a proper friendship with us and with Billy, and her poor dear mother still endeavours to keep us from harm, but they are both so afraid of Ann's father, that neither dare go against him. We are also still waiting to hear the rest of the story about Tom, but Ann's mother has not had the opportunity to return to our room and finish it.

The war is still raging, and London continues to be hit hard, but other places are also being bombed now. We just long for home, for mother and father, and most of all to feel safe and loved, like we had been before this horrible war started. Our little attic room feels more and more like a prison with the more days that pass, and because of the weather we can't even escape it to go school. However, this morning something in the house feels different, for a start there has been no shouting, but it is more than that. There is a feeling of peace and calm, but not of

53

comfort, both Eva and I can sense it, and we both feel anxious about it. What can it mean? We do not have to wait long before we discover the truth behind this mysterious feeling.

Unable to sleep further, we wash and dress quickly, but before we have finished there are footsteps coming slowly up towards the attic, but they do not belong to Ann's father. No, they are those belonging to Ann's mother, are we finally going to hear the rest of Tom's story?

The footsteps stop outside our door, but there is no knock, and she does not enter. Something is definitely wrong, but what? Eventually the footsteps begin moving back towards the little narrow staircase, before once more stopping and returning to our door. This time there is a very gentle, almost timid tap.

'Elizabeth, Eva, can I please come in? I must speak with you, it is most important.'
Having hurriedly finished dressing, Eva opens the door as I attempt to straighten the bed clothes.

'Elizabeth, leave that for now, and Eva, can you close the door please? Now come and sit beside me on the bed.'
Ann's mother pauses, swallowing hard and taking several very deep breaths before she even tries to continue.

'Now, you two girls are going to have to be very brave, and remember that whatever happens in life, you have to do your best to keep living the way that both your parents would want you to, alright?'

I can feel my chest tighten and a lump appears in my throat, my mouth goes dry and every breath seems to be a struggle. As I look across at Eva I can tell that she is feeling the same, but it is only me that says anything.

'What is it ma'am?'

The words come out, but my voice is barely more than a whisper.

'There is not an easy way for you to hear this, so I am going to be honest and say it as gently as I can.'

Glancing anxiously towards her, I can see that she too is fighting to stay in control of her feelings.

'I have received a letter this morning from your mother, and the news it contains is not what we have all been praying for.'

Gulping hard, I fear I already know what she is about to tell us, but I have to ask the question anyway.

'Is... Is it father? Has he been killed?'

'Oh Elizabeth, Eva, I wish with all my heart that I could give you a definite answer to that question, but I can't. However, your mother's letter does indeed bring news of your father, and I am afraid that he is missing

55

in action.'

We both know what news like this means from hearing other adults talk. It means that we will probably never see him again. It means that he is probably dead.

Hot salty tears are now blurring my eyes, but as I glance across towards Eva, I can see that she is just sitting, starring out of the frost-laced window.

'Eva, it will be alright, I know it will.'

I try to sound brave and positive, but the words just stick in my throat causing me to cough, and then to sob loudly and uncontrollably into my hands, before being wrapped in in a blanket and Ann's mother's arms. What am I saying? Who am I trying to convince? I don't believe that, so why should Eva?

'Hush child, you must not give up hope, your sister and your mother need you to stay strong.'

Her words are supposed to bring comfort, but they sound only hollow and empty, and the tremble in her own voice is betraying her own true feelings.

After several minutes, I manage to compose myself and once again look across at Eva. She is still sitting and starring exactly as she had been before. She has not moved or spoken at all. It is only now that Ann's mother seems to even notice.

'Eva, are you alright child? Do you understand all that I have told you?'
Still there is no reaction from my motionless sister, what is wrong with her? Now I begin to feel scared again, as neither Ann's mother or I appear to be able to get through to her at all.

'What can I do? How can I help her?'
The desperation in my voice surprises me, but I am beginning to fear that I may lose my sister as well as my dearest father.

'Now Elizabeth, both you and your sister have had a horrible shock, but you have been able to let it out, and as yet your sister just feels numb and isn't able to express it like you are. She is blanking everything out at the moment to try and protect herself, so we need to find a way of helping her to express the hurt and anger she is allowing to build up inside her. Can you think of anything which might allow her to feel secure enough to cry?'

'What about Eloise, her teddy bear that mother sent her for Christmas?'
Before Ann's mother can even begin to answer, I wriggle free from her embrace, spring off the bed and race round to Eva's side grabbing Eloise from under it, immediately putting her in Eva's hands. But still she does not move, speak or react in anyway. She looks so pale and frightened; I begin to fear she may faint.

'It's not working. Why isn't it working?'

'Calm yourself, or you will make yourself ill. I was thinking more in terms of a photograph of your father, did you bring one with you?'

This time I do not answer, instead I make my way to the small stool beside the bed and take out a small crumpled photograph from between the pages of my bible. As I see the gentle, kind face of my own dear father looking back at me, my tears begin falling once more. However, I make my way back towards Eva and, sitting myself beside her, I hold the photograph for her to see. At first, there still appears to be no reaction, and then she turns her face away clutching Eloise tightly to her before burying her head in her pillow and finally starting to sob as heartily as I had done a short while ago.

Eva continues to sob for, what seems to be a long time, but is really no longer than a few minutes, before suddenly stopping. She sits bolt upright and perfectly calmly declares to both Ann's mother and myself that she doesn't believe a word of the letter which has been read to us.

'Our father is not dead! He loves us both too much to ever leave us without saying a proper goodbye, so I will not accept these lies! Mother should not have told us such things when they cannot be true!'

'Eva, mother would never tell us lies! This is not like you, I don't want to believe it either, but we cannot pretend this hasn't happened.'

'Eva, listen to your sister please, she is right. Your mother has only passed on to you exactly what she has been told herself. You must not blame her for this. Do not forget that your father is her husband, this is as hard for her as it is for you.'

'Please Eva, we need to be able to support each other, and we can only do that if we accept that he is missing. I too hope and pray that he is still alive, but it is only the fault of the war if he isn't.'

'I don't blame mother, but this is a mistake and I will not accept it or believe it.'
I look towards my sister with great concern, before looking desperately to Ann's mother for guidance and reassurance.

'It's alright Elizabeth, Eva just needs time to come to terms with this news, but we must watch her closely, and always be here for her. Although I have never seen a reaction like this before, I am married to someone who still suffers from the results of a similar one.'

She pauses, sighing deeply and reflectively while looking to the ceiling as if asking God for strength to keep going and patience to cope.

'Please ma'am, what do you mean? I don't understand.'

'Well, I didn't think today was the right time, but in the circumstances perhaps it is better this way. I am talking about John, and his reaction to being separated from Tom for the second time. It was at this point John decided he needed a proper education that would enable him to make enough money, to own a house large enough for his own future family, as well as for his brother Tom. This really was a huge undertaking and decision for an eight year old farm boy to make. But, make it he did, with determination, a lot of hard work and many sacrifices by both him and his family, he achieved as much, if not more than he could have hoped for. Unfortunately, it has caused him to be bitter and resentful towards anyone who he considers to be less educated than himself, or those who he sees as a possible threat, which I'm afraid to say includes strangers and his own family.'

Ann's mother pauses, as if deep in thought before turning once more to look at first me, and then Eva. It is a great surprise to us both when we see the dramatic difference in Eva now. For the first time since we were told the news of our father, she appears to be really interested in all that we are being told. However, I cannot shake off the feeling that this change may not be the positive one it appears to be, could she actually be admiring Ann's father's attitude towards his family?

'Please ma'am, will you continue?'
This time it is Eva who asks the question, not me, which surprises Ann's mother as Eva is usually the quiet one of the two of us.

'Of course Eva, as you have asked so politely I will indeed continue.

John had already bought this house, and lived here for nearly three years before I even met him. Hmm, I can remember that day so clearly, but that is another story. After a few months we became engaged, and were married barely a year later. I had always lived in a small cottage until I moved in here, and Tom was not here then. I hated being alone here at first, so my parents would often visit when John was away for more than a few hours. But this just made him angry when he returned, so I had to get used to being alone.'

'Please ma'am, when did Tom come to live here?'

'Shh Eva, don't be so impatient, it is rude to interrupt.'

'It's alright Elizabeth. If you give me a moment Eva, I was just about to tell you. John spent many months after we were married searching for Tom, he had very little information to go on, so sometimes he was away for a few days. But, eventually Tom was found and John went to bring him home that very day.

It was obvious from that first day that Tom needed his brother, but John could not have imagined then exactly what challenges were ahead for all of us. Over the next few weeks Tom seemed to settle in well, but then I became pregnant with Ann, and Tom's problems began to show themselves.

At first, it was just the odd angry outburst, or occasional sign of panic, usually when a door slammed or someone entered the room and made Tom jump. But quite soon his behaviour and sudden changes in mood began to cause us both much concern. John tried to talk to Tom about perhaps speaking to a doctor to get some help, but this only seemed to make things worse. These changes in Tom caused John much heartache and sorrow; he even began to blame himself for bringing Tom to live here. But, I tried to ease this burden, by explaining to John that he had no way of knowing quite how the horrors of war could change a person so drastically. I also began to ask what Tom used to be like, so that I may get to know a bit more about him. At first John was reluctant to tell me anything, because he considered it to be of concern to his family only. However, after I explained that both I and the baby were his family now too, he relented and a picture of the younger

Tom began to develop.

He had been a mild-mannered, loving, peaceful boy, always wanting to help in any way he could, and was utterly devoted to his younger brother. So, it was sad to see how war had changed him so dramatically into a withdrawn, hard-hearted, and at times terrifying man. Occasionally, his angry outbursts were now becoming violent and getting much harder to cope with. In between these times we did begin to see glimpses of the old of the old Tom, particularly after Ann was first born. He could calm and settle her better than either of us could. But that all changed in one single day. A gun went off in the distance and Tom retreated to his room, hardly able to leave it from that day to this, and the old Tom has not even been glimpsed since.

However, he is still John's brother, so he continues to live here, but still he barely leaves his room, and the door is kept locked at his request.'

'Has Ann ever seen him since she was a baby?'

'Yes Elizabeth, Ann met him once, on one of the rare occasions that he wanted to walk in the garden. He seems to find some peace there at times, and always has his window open, even in the worst of winter. But she was so frightened by him that we have to ensure that she is not at home now if he does choose to venture out.'

Hearing a stifled sniff, I glance anxiously towards Eva; tears are glistening in her eyes once more.

'What's wrong Eva? I thought you wanted to hear the rest of Tom's story as much as I did?'

'I did, but now I'm frightened.'

'What are you frightened of Eva? Tom cannot and would not hurt you, we have made quite certain of that, besides, he would probably be more frightened of you than you are of him, because strangers have always caused him to be nervous ever since I've known him.'

'I'm sorry ma'am, but it is not Tom that frightens me.'

'Whatever is it then child? Please tell me so that I can help you.'

Her sobs are louder now and her words more heartfelt and desperate than before. My own eyes are also becoming blurry again.

'You can't help, you can't!'

'Please Eva; won't you at least let me try? What are you so frightened of?'

'I am frightened that when our own dear father does come home, he will be like Tom. I couldn't bear that, I just couldn't!'

I gasp. Finding myself hardly able to breathe, I have not even thought of that, but now could this be the reality we are to face? This is even harder to comprehend than the possibility of never seeing him again. I too am sobbing once more and do not even hear the footsteps on the stairs approaching the attic. It is not until the door opens and Ann's father enters that I even lift my head from the pillow. When I see who is standing there, I feel myself stiffen all over and prepare to be shouted at, if not beaten. But something about him is different, and when he doesn't speak, I dare to look again.

His face is nearly white, instead of the usual redness that we are so used to seeing, and he looks as though he too could cry at any minute. This is even more surprising because I never thought that men would cry, especially this one!

Removing her arms from around us, she quickly stands and moves across the room to stand beside her husband, taking his arm as if to stop him collapsing.

'John, what is it? What is wrong? You look awful, are you ill? Is it Ann? Please tell me.'

'Ann is fine, and I am not ill.'
His voice is faltering and hollow, but his tone is still as sharp and severe as always.

'Well what is it then, you look as though you have seen a ...'

'Don't say it, just don't! I have just

65

been to check on Tom, and he is not there.'

Ann's mother's face has now gone as white as her husbands, and they just stand looking at each other until she recovers herself enough to speak.

'What do you mean he is not there? Where is he? How did he get out?'

'I don't know. The door was locked as it always is, but when I entered the room, I was met with an icy blast. His window was wide open and he had gone. I looked out of the window, but couldn't see him anywhere. I don't know what to do, he is just so vulnerable. If I go to the local station to notify the police and they approach him, it will just frighten him and we both know what could happen then.'

'Oh John, what can I do to help? Where would he go?'

'I don't know, but he has started talking about the farm again, if he goes there I dare not even think about what will happen. My sister barely knew him when he was a boy, and has certainly not seen him since he returned to live with us; at least I don't think she has?'

Ann's father was now looking hard at his wife as if he were accusing her of something.

'Don't even think it John, I know how protective you are of him, and I can assure you that she has not been here while I've been at home.'

Ann's mother's voice is far more insistent than we have heard before, and even her husband seems slightly shocked. Eva and I are now sitting huddled together on the bed, partly for comfort and security, and partly for warmth.

'We should not be discussing this here; Eva and Elizabeth have got enough to cope with this morning, they don't need to be worried by this as well John.'

Both Ann's parents leave our room and descend the stairs to the main landing below. Continuing to huddle together, we sit in stunned silence still sniffing with tears ready to start falling again as we hear two sets of footsteps approach and enter Tom's room below. After all that we have been told about Tom, are we still safe here?

After several minutes we hear Ann's parents leave Tom's room again, and descend the main staircase.

'Elizabeth, do you think Tom will be alright?'

It is not the croakiness in my sister's voice that surprises me, but the question she has just asked.

'Why do you ask Eva? Why does this concern you so much?'

'I... I don't know really, I suppose it is because of father being missing and the

67

possibility that he might come back like Tom. If we can't help father, perhaps we can help Tom?'

'Oh Eva, I don't know. Do you really believe that we could help Tom? Surely we would be interfering, and we could just make matters worse. You heard what Ann's father said about the police, we are strangers, he hasn't even seen us, and we could find ourselves in real danger!'

'I know, but shouldn't we at least try?'
I don't know what to say, but I am pleased to see something of the real Eva shining through again, she has always had a heart for people. So, in spite of any fear I maybe feeling we both head downstairs, which in itself could be risky as Ann's father has made it obvious we are not welcome, especially downstairs. But, the reception we receive is much warmer than we could have imagined or hoped for.

It is Ann's mother, who speaks first, but her father does not seem to resent our presence as he has done before, perhaps he is aware of the content of the letter from mother? Or perhaps he is just too worried about Tom to worry about us at all? Whatever it is, it makes a welcome change from our usual experience of him.

'Please, come in girls, are you alright? Can we help you in anyway?'

'Please ma'am; we would like to offer

our help to you if we can?'

'Why Eva, whatever do you mean?'

'Well, we know we can't help our father at the moment, so we thought that perhaps we could help Tom. We don't want to interfere, but we could see how concerned and worried you both are, and thought perhaps we could help find him?'

Ann's father says nothing, but looks at us as if he doesn't know quite what to think.

'Oh girls, your offer is greatly appreciated, but I think it would be better for you to stay here with Ann and keep her company. We don't know where to even start looking, and besides, we have no idea how he would react to two small girls that he has never seen before. You could find yourselves in great danger.'

'We just thought that because we know how it feels to be frightened and lost, we might be able to make him feel better. But if staying with Ann will help, we can do that.'

Now it is Ann's father who speaks, but in a very different way to the one we are used to.

'Thank you girls, I really do appreciate your concern but Agnes is right, you are better to stay here with Ann. She could really use your friendship at the moment, and I know that you could do with some cheering up yourselves. When I thought my brother had died, it was as if my whole world fell apart, so I can understand a little of what you must be feeling.'

For the first time since we arrived here, Ann's father is being almost kind, so we decide it is best to just accept what we have been told.

'Thank you, but please let us help if we can.'

'You already have, more than you can know. Now, off you go and find Ann, I think she may still be in her room, she is so afraid of her uncle that she dare not come out at the moment.'

Leaving the lounge we make our way back up the main staircase and go straight to Ann's room. We knock gently and wait for her to answer. There is a long pause, and we are just about to knock again, when we hear her moving towards the door.

'Who is it?'

Her voice is little more than a whisper, but remembering how frightened she is of Tom, we are not surprised.

'It's alright Ann, it is only us, can we come in please?'

'Yes of course, but what about father? You know what he said about us being friends.'

'It's alright, he knows we are here. He has been really nice to us this morning.'

As she closes the door behind us, even Ann

70

looks surprised.

'I think it is because he is too worried about Tom to be nasty to us.'

'Eva, you shouldn't say things like that. He really did try to make us both feel better this morning, and you know it!'

'I suppose you're right Elizabeth, but I don't think I will ever feel better until father comes home.'

Ann looks at us with a confused expression on her face. She obviously does not know about our mother's latest letter.

'What do you mean Eva? Has something happened to your father Elizabeth? Please tell me, that is what friends are for, to share your troubles with.'

I can feel tears burning the back of my eyes again, but manage to swallow hard and stop them from falling, at least for now.

'Oh Ann, your mother received a letter from our mother this morning, and it says that our father is missing in action.'

'Oh... Oh I am so sorry, does that mean that he is...'

'If you are asking whether he is dead or not, we don't know, and that makes it even harder to believe. Eva is refusing to believe it at all, but I don't know what to think.'

Eva stares at me as though I am betraying our father even talking about it, but then she turns to Ann.

'It is not that I don't believe that he is missing, I just refuse to believe that we will never see him again. I know that our father will come back, I just know he will, because he would not leave us forever without saying goodbye first.'

Ann looks at both of us, her grey-green eyes wide, as if terrified by something she has seen.

'Ann, what is it? You look awful.'

'I was just thinking how awful it must be for both of you, I cannot begin to think how I would feel if it was my father. I know he can be severe at times, but he is my father, and I do love him very much.'

'Of course you do, and he is very worried about his brother at the moment.'

'I know, but my Uncle Tom scares me, he is so tall and stern, he looks like a giant.'

'Is that why he scares you so much?'

'Well, that is not the only reason, he never says very much, but when he does speak he shouts. I hear him sometimes when father and mother go into his room.'

'Have you ever heard what he is saying?'

'Not exactly Eva because I am too far away, all I usually hear is a lot of shouting. It is hard to pick out many words, but he does seem to blame father for something I think.'

'What do you mean Ann?'

72

'I don't know exactly, but it seems to have something to do with the farm where Billy lives.'

A cold shiver runs down my back, could Tom have gone to the farm? Are Billy and his family safe if he has? Will Ann's father even go there to look? Before I can ask Ann any of these questions, she begins to talk in a different way from before.

'Father hasn't been to the farm for ages. He won't, because it would mean talking to his sister and her family.'

'Ann, do you think your uncle could find his way to the farm from here?'

'I don't know, but he probably could, he lived here as a child until he ran away to war, but why would he want to? According to father, his sister is as scared of him as I am.'

'Is she really, or do you think that your father has just told you that?'

'I... I don't know, father doesn't tell lies but maybe he believes that she is, because of the way his parents treated Tom all those years ago.'

For several minutes the three of us just sit looking at each other on the floor of Ann's room, not really knowing what to think, say or do. Then Ann says something that surprises both Eva and I.

'Sometimes I feel guilty for not seeing my uncle, and wonder if, perhaps he is scared too. I think he feels a lot of hurt and pain from when he went to war. But when I said this to father he just shouted and told me not to mention it again. I can't help thinking that he might just need a friend to talk too.'

Eva and I just sit and look at each other, before Eva responds in a way that is typical of her.

'I think you are right Ann, and I think that we should go and find him anyway. We can help him, I know we can.'

'Eva, we have been told to stay here, we must not disobey Ann's parents, that is not what mother would want, both of us know that.'

'You are right Elizabeth, I know you are, but mother isn't here, and I just want to help.'

'I know, so do I, but to go out in this weather, looking for a total stranger who could be dangerous cannot be the best thing to do.'

'No Elizabeth, Eva is right; we can't just sit here and do nothing. Mother has always told me that when I was a baby, Uncle Tom loved me dearly, and enjoyed nothing more than holding me in his arms while I slept. Maybe I am the one who can really help him.'

I cannot believe what I am hearing, and a growing sense of fear is already building inside me, but there is also a real sense of adventure. For the first time since we left London, I am beginning to feel as if we are starting to belong. I never thought that this would be possible here, but, just maybe things are changing for us. However, I still feel as though we are being disobedient, and that I should at least try to dissuade Eva and Ann from this course of action.

'Are you sure we shouldn't just stay here and wait? Maybe your parents will ask for our help later?'

'I doubt it, father would never ask for my help. No, I think we should go now, maybe Billy can help too?'

'But... I still think...'

'You don't have to come with us if you're too scared, but if you stay here you'll have to keep out of sight and not go telling on us.'

It is obvious that they have decided to go anyway, so, even though I still doubt the wisdom of this decision, I reluctantly agree to go with them. After all, I cannot imagine how I could explain their absence if I were caught alone at the house without telling the truth. Eva and I return to the attic to put on our warmest clothes, which will still offer rather limited warmth against weather as harsh as this, but before we can leave the attic again, Ann is at our door.

'Aren't you two ready yet? If we don't hurry and leave now, mother and father are bound to find out and stop us!'

I say nothing, but cannot help thinking that perhaps that would be a good thing. However, it appears that Eva on the other hand, cannot wait to get started but this is not like her at all. She is usually the cautious one, not me.

'Oh do hurry Elizabeth, unless you want us to get caught, and probably beaten too.'

The tone of her voice and expression on her face show me all too clearly that she knows what I am thinking, after all as twins this is almost inevitable as we have a special link and bond with each other. But it also gives her own feelings away too. She is scared but will not admit it! Without another word spoken between any of us, we make our way downstairs as quietly as we can. First from the attic, avoiding the squeaky stair, and then down the main staircase.

My heart is thumping really hard now, and with every step we take I become more and more certain that we should not be doing this. We finally reach the bottom of the stairs and instead of heading to the front door, Ann beckons to us to follow her towards the back of the house.

'Come on, it is better if we go this way,

mother and father will hear the front door and stop us before we even reach the gate. But, if we go the back way, they won't know we have gone until it is too late to stop us.'

Now my feeling of uncertainty is even stronger, it is obvious that Ann knows we are doing the wrong thing by all that she has just said, but if I don't go with them, I shudder to think what might happen. At least if I am there, I might be able to persuade them not to do anything too silly or dangerous. So, with this hope in my heart, I follow Ann and Eva out into a large and wonderful garden. Even covered with a thick blanket of snow its beauty is very obvious.

'Isn't this beautiful Elizabeth, it is like a winter wonderland.'

'Yes...Yes it is.'

We both stand and absorb the beauty of our surroundings for a few seconds before Ann's rather shrill voice brings us back to reality with a jolt.

'We haven't got time to admire the scenery; we've got to find Tom!'

'But it is beautiful, don't you think so Ann?'

'I suppose so, I haven't really thought about it, now come on or we will get caught.'

Her reaction is surprising to both of us, but then I suppose if you see something everyday it isn't quite the same. The urgency of Ann's voice is obvious, and even I find myself getting caught up in the excitement of what we are doing.

We are not out for long, before we are all feeling cold and much less certain than when we left the house. It has started to snow again too, but there is something strangely beautiful and peaceful about walking through falling snow.

'At least the snow will cover up our footsteps, so mother and father won't be able to follow us.'

Unsure whether this is a good thing or a bad thing, I answer her without mentioning that fact at all.

'True, but it will also cover any footsteps which Tom might have left, so we can't follow him either.'

'I hadn't thought of that, it could make finding him more difficult than I hoped it would be.'

'Well, didn't you say he had been talking about the farm a lot recently? Shouldn't we head towards there? At least it would be somewhere to start.'

'Eva is right Ann, but do you know where it is? How do we get to it from here?'

Ann eventually stops walking and stands looking thoughtful for several minutes before answering us.

'What is it Ann? Are you lost?'

'No that's just it, I'm not lost, but I am a bit nervous to tell you what I am thinking.'

'Why? It can't be that bad surely? Just tell us before we all freeze to death.'

'Well, there are two ways to get to the farm from here, one is to go along the road, but that would be too obvious and I don't think Tom would want to be seen.'

'Yes, we know that way, Billy brought us back to your house by the road. I think you are probably right about Tom though, if he doesn't like leaving his room, he isn't going to want to be seen by anyone. What is the other way?'

Even as these last few words leave my mouth I regret them, my thoughts flash back to that night and I can remember Billy saying something about some woods. I can also remember his mother saying that they weren't safe. However, it was dark then, and it is light now. This thought is supposed to console me, but it doesn't really work. Then, another even stranger and more concerning thought hits me, if Tom doesn't like to leave his room, what on earth would persuade him to leave the house? Before I can ponder on this point for long, Ann is tugging at my sleeve to attract my attention.

'Elizabeth, are you alright? You look as if you are miles away.'

But before I can answer her, she is off again,

this time staring hard at me.

'Now you are both listening, I will tell you about the other way to the farm. We have to follow the path through the woods, and I have only ever been through there once that I can remember, and that was with mother. But, that will be safer for us, and is far more likely to be the way that Tom went.'

Eva and I look at each other, and then at Ann. For the first time since leaving the house, Eva and I appear to be feeling the same way.

'Well, are we going to find Tom or not?'

Ann's voice is so indignant, that before we know what is happening, we find ourselves agreeing to follow her into the woods.

The snow is falling really fast now, and it is getting hard to see where we are going, let alone find a footpath to follow, we don't even know whether we are going in the same direction. But, turning back is not an option, so we just keep going. Eva and I would definitely get lost without Ann, and it would be very wrong of us to leave her alone, so continue we must. By now we are in the middle of the woods, and although it is daylight, the trees are so dense here that it looks almost dark. This is not helped by the greyness of a snow-filled sky. However, this denseness does mean that the snow isn't getting in our eyes quite so much, as it is getting caught in the trees rather than reaching the ground. It is also easier to walk through here, as the snow under foot is not so deep.

Eva and I are so intent on watching where we are walking, that we nearly knock Ann over.

'Ouch! Careful, didn't you see me?'

'Sorry Ann, we were looking at the ground so we didn't trip, we didn't notice that you had stopped.'

'Why have you stopped?'

'I don't really know Eva, I suddenly felt as though we were being watched, or even followed.'

'Well, we were walking behind you, so technically we were following you.'

'Yes, but you weren't watching me or you wouldn't have walked into me. But never mind that now, it wasn't you anyway, it sounded like something at the side of us, but taking great care to remain hidden.'

'We can't hear anything now Ann, could it have been Tom?'

'Possibly, but it didn't sound big enough for him, it was more like someone our size, or even an animal of some kind. Oh well, they seem to have gone now, let's get moving, I'm getting hungry so it must be nearly lunchtime.'

It is only now that we realise that we have got nothing to eat or drink. I can just imagine what mother would say if she was here. I say nothing about this to Eva and I try to push it from my own mind, but without much success. Up ahead Ann has stopped again, but this time we can see why. The falling snow which had initially been almost a comfort, has become almost eerie and threatening now, and now we face another dilemma.

'Now, which way do we go?'

'Don't you have any idea Ann?'

'I told you I had only been through here once, but I'm sure that whichever way we choose we will find the farm eventually.'

'Aren't you scared Ann?'

'No way, this is the most fun I have ever had. Father would never let me do anything like this.'

I say nothing, but know only too well that our father would not let us do something like this either. Unable to hold back anymore a heartfelt sigh escapes my lips. Eva makes no reply, but her own misery is all too visible.

Having stood, staring into the woods in both directions for several minutes, we all agree and decide to follow the path to the left. Our main reasons for this are that the woods don't look as dense that way, and that from Ann's house, the road would take us to the farm in that direction. If we really thought about this, we would soon realise that, as we are, by now completely lost anyway, this makes no more sense than going to the right. But, having made a decision, we finally get walking again.

By now the icy cold is really beginning to hurt our face, hands and feet, but not one of us is prepared to admit this to the other two. However, after only a short while our moods are lifted as we reach the edge of the woods, the only problem is, that there is no sign of the farm or Tom anywhere.

'Eva, I am sure that the farm was really close to the woods, so why can't we see it?'

'I don't know, but this road still looks almost familiar. I don't like this, I wish we hadn't come.'

Eva looks as though she is about to start crying, but saying that I thought this would happen, is not going to help. Even Ann has become quiet; in fact she looks quiet pale.

'Ann, are you alright? You look really pale.'

'Oh Elizabeth, I'm beginning to think that perhaps you were right after all, we should never have come looking for Tom alone. Will you ever forgive me for being so selfish?'

Now it is my turn to feel guilty as I realise that her eagerness to find Tom, was actually the most unselfish thing she could do. She has always been scared of her uncle, and today she is showing real love and concern for him, and for her father.

Realising that one of us has to decide what our next move should be, I take a deep breath and say the one thing that I never thought I would say.

'Well, if the farm is not here, we must go back the way we came, and follow the other path until it too comes out of the woods.'

Both Eva and Ann look at me with such expressions of horror, that for a few seconds I fear they may have seen or heard something that I have missed.

'You mean we have to go back into the woods? It has taken us so long to get out of them already.'

'Well, have you got any better ideas Eva?'
My reply is harsher than I had intended, but I really cannot see any other choice.

'I hate to say it Eva, but I fear Elizabeth may be right.'
Then we hear it, chiming twelve times.

'It's the clock on the church Elizabeth; don't you remember it from the day we arrived?'

'Yes, yes I do.'

'Then it's alright, we don't have to go

back through the woods?'

For a short while we all feel relieved, but then I remember that the church is a long way from Ann's house, and even further from the farm.

'I'm sorry, but we still have to go back through the woods, the church is the other end of the village from where we need to be.'

'Elizabeth is right Ann, we have no choice.'

Reluctantly the three of us turn round and begin our journey back the way we have just come into the woods.

We soon reach the point where the path divides, so we continue straight on along in the direction which we avoided before because of the dense trees. The trees are certainly bigger and closer together this way, making it seem almost black beneath them. But at least the snow has stopped falling, and there is even a very weak, watery-looking sun trying to break through the thick, grey, heavy cloak of cloud which has surrounded us all morning. However, this small chink of brightness has little to no effect on the gloom under the trees; neither does it have any effect on the chill of this winter.

Despite the denseness of the trees, we quickly find ourselves at the edge of the woods once again. This time the farmhouse can be clearly seen, and the welcome sight of smoke rising from the chimney even encourages us to quicken our pace a little. In fact until we reach the doorway, we have almost forgotten why we are here. Then, just as we are about to knock, all three of us freeze, remembering the reason for our visit.

'What if Tom isn't here? What if he never made it this far? What if...'

'Don't say it Ann, we must have covered every inch of those woods, and we have found nothing. If he isn't here, we will go back by road and see if we can find him that way.'

'Oh Elizabeth, I don't even know if my aunt will want to see me, father has been so unkind for so long, that I fear she may not even want to know me.'

'I cannot believe that Billy's mother could ever be like that to anyone after the warm welcome we received on our first visit here.'

'Yes, but that was different, you went as friends of Billy, I have barely even spoken to him, and even when I have, I was horrible to him.'

'Well, either we knock on the door and see if Tom is here, or we have come all this way for nothing. I'm not scared!'

'Eva, wait! What are you going to say when the door is opened? How are we going to explain our presence here, and why we disobeyed Ann's parents?'

Now it is not just Ann who is scared, but I too am beginning to doubt whether we should even be here. But Eva doesn't seem to want to listen to reason, and before we can stop her, she knocks firmly on the door. Ann and I are almost ready to run straight back into the woods, but the friendly, rosy-cheeked face of Billy's mother is a welcome sight after our long, cold journey.

'Well, I'll be, whatever have we got here? What on earth are you three girls doing out in weather like this? Oh Ann, does your father know you are here? Come in, come in all of you, you must be hungry, and you will certainly be cold and tired.'

'I... I didn't know if you would even want to see me because of how my father has treated ...'

'Oh my dear child, we don't bear grudges here, it is lovely to see you all, but why are you here? Today of all days.'

As we all huddle together in the kitchen, partly for warmth, and partly for courage, Billy's mother presents each of us with a bowl of hot stew, and a large chunk of freshly baked bread. Eva and I sit down at the kitchen table and tuck in eagerly, but Ann takes much gentle persuasion before she even picks up the spoon. But eventually, even she too has an empty bowl in front of her.

'Right, now you are fed and warm, would one of you like to tell me why you are here?'

Ann and I look at each other and remain silent. Eva, on the other hand, still seems full of excitement and determination, and surprises us both as she begins to tell the whole story. Even Billy's mother is surprised, because last time we were here, Eva barely said a word.

'Well, this morning Elizabeth and I got a letter from our mother, or rather Ann's mother did, and it said our father is missing. Elizabeth thinks he is dead, but I know he isn't. Anyway, while we were in our room with Ann's mother, her husband came in said that Tom was missing, so we have come to find him.'

'Wait! Just slow down a bit, first can I say how sorry I am about your father, this must be a very hard time for you both. Now, what do you mean that Tom is missing?'

Before Eva can start her excited babbling again, I decide that perhaps I ought to try to explain.

'Well, Eva is right, Ann's father did come into our room and say that Tom was missing, I can still see his terribly worried expression. When he said this, Ann's mother took his arm to comfort him, and they went downstairs together. I fear that he thinks his brother is at great risk, or even dead. After they left, Eva suggested that maybe we should offer to help find him. I was uncertain about this from the start, but we went downstairs to where Ann's parents were, and offered anyway. We were both surprised when they thanked us for our offer, but told us instead to go and find Ann and keep her company.'

'So why have you ended up here?'
Billy's mother is looking and sounding increasingly concerned now, but I decide that she should know everything, so I continue.

'Well, when we first got to Ann's room, she was frightened to open the door, in case her uncle was about. But eventually she let's us in and we begin talking about our news from mother, about Tom, about our father, and after a while Ann and Eva decide that we should help with the search anyway. I try to stop them, I don't want to disobey Ann's parents, but they are so determined to come that I think I ought to come with them anyway.'

'You girls really should have stayed at home; I know you think you are helping, but Ann, now your parents will be worried about you too.'

'I hadn't thought of that, but I never get to do anything exciting, so we sneaked out of the back door so we wouldn't get caught.'

'Yes, I guessed that, but why have you come here?'

This time it is Ann who takes over and continues to explain our story.

'I never saw Tom, but I could often hear him arguing with father, and recently he has mentioned the farm a lot. So, we decide that this would be the best place to start looking. We have come through the woods so we wouldn't be seen, and because we thought he would come that way too. But we kept getting lost and ended up on the wrong side to start with, so we had to come all the way back to get here.'

Billy's mother's usually rosy cheeks have gone quite pale now, and she looks as if she can't say anything. Then, after a long pause, she gets up from the table and walks over to the large window.

'I... I never really knew my oldest brother, and your father never wanted me to visit. So, I have spent all these years getting used to the fact that we would never have the chance to know each other. Why would he come here?'

'I don't know, it is just that he was always shouting at father about it, so I didn't know where else to start looking.'

Ann looks as if she is about to start crying, but Billy's mother is quickly beside her.

'Come, come child, none of this is your

fault, but I'm afraid your journey here is wasted. Tom is not here, and I very much doubt whether he will come here. Our parents sent him away, so his last memories of here must be painful ones. Now, you girls listen to me, you are to go straight home along the road from here. It will be getting dark soon, and I wouldn't want you out in the dark in weather like this.'

'But what about Tom? We really need to find him; he must be so frightened on his own?'

'Now listen to me, if Tom should come here, he will receive the same welcome as you have, and we will make sure he is safe. So, you must promise to go straight home alright?'

Looking at each other the three of us agree, and get ready to leave, but before we do Eva has to ask where Billy is.

'Billy is helping his pa on the farm, the animals really suffer in weather like this and we need all the help we can get.'

'Can we stay and help too? Then if Tom should come here, we will know and he can come back with us.'

'Eva! We really should go back to Ann's and wait for him there, besides he could have gone home by now.'

'Don't you want to stay here and help with the animals Elizabeth?'

'Now girls, farm work is hard and sometimes dangerous, this weather just increases the risks and makes it harder. It is not that I am not grateful for your offer, it is just that you are not used to farm life, and the work needs the strength of men and boys.'

'But I am strong; please may I stay and help? I don't want to go back!'

'Eva, you shouldn't say things like that, it makes you sound ungrateful and I know that you are not that. You are welcome here anytime, but I really must insist that you return to Ann's house now before it gets dark, please.'

There is a hint of fear in Billy's mother's voice now, is it because she is scared of Tom, or is it Ann's father that frightens her more? Either way, our continued presence here only seems to be adding to her worries.

'Come on Eva, please don't make a fuss, besides it could be fun.'

I cannot imagine why Ann would consider the walk home along the road as being fun, but it seemed to encourage Eva a little, so without any further delay we leave the warmth of the farmhouse and begin making our way to the road. Then, before either Ann or I can stop her, Eva darts off to the left towards an old tumbledown barn which obviously no longer used.

'Eva! Wait! Where are you going

now? The road is this way.'

Eva doesn't even seem to hear me, but Ann turns to look at me before turning away again and following Eva towards the barn. Left standing alone, halfway between the farmhouse and the road, I feel like crying, all I want is the soft, warm comforting embrace of our own mother. Nevertheless, having decided that they are not coming back, I make up my mind that the only thing to do is follow them. However, the closer I get to the old barn, the more uncomfortable that place is making me feel. By the time I reach the entrance, both Ann and Eva are already inside and because of the gloom, I can barely see them.

Knowing that we have no right to be here, and feeling as though we are intruding, when I speak it is little more than a whisper.

'We really shouldn't be here, it doesn't even look safe! Please wait for me; I think we should at least stay together.'

'Shush Elizabeth! Listen, can you hear anything above us?'

'There's no-one here but us, I'm sure of it.'

I say this as confidently as I can, trying to convince myself as much as the other two, but every plank and joint in the old place seems to be creaking and moaning in the icy wind which is now blowing harder than before.

'That's not true, that's why I came. I saw a tall dark figure come in here, but now I can't find him.'

A cold shiver runs down my back.

'Him? How do you know it was a man?'

At that moment boards above our heads begin to creak and dust begins to fall thickly, getting into our eyes and throats, making it difficult to see or talk. In fact, when we try all we do is cough. Then, there is a loud crack followed by a loud a thud as boards give way, and something hit's the ground only a short distance behind where we are all standing.

'Quick, come on we need to get out of here it's not safe! It is falling down and if we don't go now we will be trapped underneath it.'

I begin tugging at Eva's coat sleeve desperately trying to get her to come with me, but she just shrugs me off. So, feeling more and more desperate with every second that passes, I try to get to Ann see sense.

'Ann, please we must go now!'

'We can't just go Elizabeth, something or someone just fell through those boards, we should at least se if they are alright.'

'I suppose you're right, but we must hurry or the whole barn could collapse on top of us all.'

To begin with the heap on the floor just

looks like a load of old rags and sacks, but as we move closer, we can see that it is a man.

'Do you think he's...?'

'Do I think he's what Eva?'

'Do you think he's dead? Is that what you were going to say Eva?'

'Yes...Yes Ann it is. He fell a long way, and he isn't moving, who do you think he is?'

'How do I know? I haven't seen his face yet!'

We continue to creep closer hardly daring to breath in case we scare him, or is it because we are scared ourselves? Ann reaches him first and bends over his head gently lifting the hood of his coat so we can see who he is, and to check if he is breathing or not. But before Eva or I can see anything, Ann jumps up and scurries quickly back to us gasping as she does so.

'Ann whatever is the matter? Do you know who he is? Is he...'

'Don't say it Elizabeth please, don't. We have just found my uncle, this is Tom. Please help him, please!'

These words send a shiver all the way down my back. Our search is over, this is what we set out to do, but part of me now is wishing we hadn't found him, at least, not like this.

'Eva, run back to the house and tell Billy's mother that we have found Tom. Tell her that he is hurt and we need help. Go on, quickly!'

'But why do I have to go? Why can't you or Ann go?'

'Just do it Eva, don't argue! We must try and help Tom, but we can't do it alone, and after all, you are the reason we are still here! So GO!'

'Please Eva; you said you wanted to help.'

'I do, but... oh very well.'

I watch as Eva turns and makes her way, grudgingly back across the barn towards the entrance, and then begin her short journey back towards the farmhouse. I turn back to look at Ann who still appears to be in shock and unaware of exactly what is happening.

'Right Ann, while we are waiting we should at least try to make him more comfortable and keep him warm.'

'How? We are cold enough ourselves, and I can't see any blankets or anything in here that we can use Elizabeth.'

'I know, I wish it wasn't so gloomy, I can't see very much either, but there must be something we can use, even if it is just some old straw. Do you want to stay with Tom while I have a look? He knows you, and if, I mean when he wakes up it would be better if he saw a face he recognised.'

'Oh must I, he still scares me, and besides I haven't seen him for years, what makes you think he will know me?'

'Well, he certainly won't know me, he hasn't ever seen me before, and someone really should stay with him.'

'Alright, but please don't be too long, and don't go too far will you?'

'I will still be in the barn Ann, but I must try and find something in here we can use.'

Ann comes over to kneel beside her uncle and I begin to search for anything that might be useful. I make my way carefully and slowly to the back of the old building, and following the wall, I search slowly round the whole place. Taking each corner in turn, but there doesn't appear to be anything in here at all. Then, just as I am about to check the last corner, Ann calls to me with real fear in her voice.

'Elizabeth, Elizabeth, come quickly, I think I heard something.'

'Wait a minute, I am just about finished, I only have this last corner and side to check, but I haven't been able to find anything.'

'Please Elizabeth, I think the noise I heard is coming from Tom.'

'What? How can any noise come from someone who is not awake?'

By the time I finish speaking, I am once again at Ann's side. Now we are both kneeling beside Tom listening intently. For several minutes we don't hear anything, but then, there it is, the faintest noise I have ever heard, and this time it is not just the once, but several times. Each time we hear it, it seems to get a little louder.

'Ann, you are right, I can hear it too, this has to be a good sign because dead people don't make noises do they? Maybe he is starting to wake up, and Eva must be back at the farmhouse by now. Why don't you go and see if anyone is coming?'

'Are you sure you will be alright? I won't leave the barn, I promise.'

I assure her that I will be perfectly alright alone for such a short while, although deep down I am doubting the truth of these words myself, so I don't think she is convinced by my false confidence either. She reaches the barn's entrance, peers out, but says nothing.

'Can you see anyone coming Ann?'

'I… I don't know, I can't see very much at all.'

Now I really begin to get frightened, as I realise the gloom in the barn seems to be getting worse, and I can hardly see Ann standing only feet away from me at the entrance to the barn.

'What do you mean Ann? You must be able to see something?'

'Well, I fear that my aunt was right, it

98

is getting dark and the snow is falling really fast again.'

'Oh no, I hope Eva got back to the farm alright? Well, we will just have to stay here until help comes. It will come soon Ann, I promise.'

But, even as Ann returns to her place next to me on the floor of the barn, I can see from her expression that I am even less convincing than I thought I was. After only another few minutes, we can no longer even see each other or Tom. Any light has all but gone, and the gloominess of the barn is replaced with a thick cloak of blackness which is almost choking in its intensity. My eyes are beginning to feel heavy with tiredness now too, but I know that I must not give in to sleep. Anyway, I doubt the fear that I am feeling would let me sleep for very long.

'Ann, are you awake?'

'Of course, I wouldn't dare go to sleep in here, and besides I am far to cold to sleep.'

She's right, I adjust my position slightly to try and get more comfortable, but I am rapidly losing all feeling in my hands and feet, and I have got pins and needles in my legs where I have had them curled up underneath me. A strong gust of wind blows through the barn and the intense cold hits me like shards of icy water.

'How much longer do you think they'll

be?'

I was dreading Ann asking this question, because I didn't have an answer, only more questions that I hardly dare think about. The more time that passes, the less certain I become that Eva even made it back to the farmhouse to raise the alarm. Now I find myself worrying about her, if she didn't make it back, where is she? Is she lying hurt somewhere? What has happened to her? What is going to happen to us if they don't know where we are? With these questions whirling so intensely around my head I can barely think, but I must try to find an answer to Ann's question that will both comfort and encourage her as well as me. But how? What can I say at a time like this?

'I'm sure they'll be here soon, they won't leave us out here for much longer.'
But even as I say the words, they sound hollow and unreal, is our situation really that hopeless?
Ann and I sit huddled together beside her Uncle Tom, who remains motionless for what feels like hours, but in truth barely an hour has passed since Eva went for help. Then, our first sign of hope, voices can be heard in the distance but they get closer and are definitely approaching the barn. Eva must have made it after all. Then the beam from a torch can be seen penetrating the darkness that surrounds

us, before a voice calls out to us from the barns entrance.

'Ann, Elizabeth are you alright?'
I recognize it at once as the voice of Billy's father.

'Yes we are alright now, we are over here, we are just glad that you have come to help us. Is Eva with you?'

'No, she has stayed back at the house with Joan and the girls. I am sorry we took so long to get here, but your sister only told us where you were after she had stopped crying and shivering. Sopping wet she was when she got back to the house.'

'How did she get so wet? It wasn't snowing when she left.'

'No, it wasn't, but she managed to fall over in the snow, and our Billy found her when I sent him back for his tea.'

'Well where was she? The house isn't that far from here, and she knew we needed help urgently!'

'I'm afraid that she might not have gone towards the house straight away, she said that she had wanted to find Billy first.'
Seeing the look of annoyance and hurt on my face, Billy's father continues.

'Don't you be too hard on her, she has already been given a talking to by my wife, so I don't think she'll be doing her own thing again in a hurry.'

Smiling, Billy's father bent down beside us and looked carefully at Tom. He will need to be carried back to the farm carefully, his injuries are bad, but he looks strong so don't you two go giving up hope alright?'

'Oh, we won't, I know he will be better soon, he has to be, my father will blame me if he isn't.'

'Now Ann, why would you be thinking such a thing as that?'

'He will blame me because I went against him and came to find Tom myself. He will say that the fright we gave him made him fall.'

'Don't you worry your pretty little head about your father; I think you may be surprised. I know you did wrong, but if you were my girl I'd be right proud of someone who was as brave and caring as you have been.'

'Thank you, but I'm not your daughter, and you really don't know my father.'

By now the two farmhands who had come with Billy's father had carefully lifted Tom and begun walking slowly back across the barn towards the entrance.

'Come on you two, you both need a hot drink and something to eat before we decide how to get you home.'

Without another word, we gratefully accept this invitation and follow behind the others with Billy's father holding us close to him to shield us against the weather.

Part
3

Despite our worst fears, the reaction of Ann's parents was very different from what we had expected. Although they had been angry that we had disobeyed them, they were overwhelmed with relief that we were all safe and that Tom had been found.

Tom is still recovering at the farm, only now, a fractured, hurting family was, for the first time in years, beginning to communicate again. A healing has started, and it is Ann's father who has thanked us for our courage and help more than once. We have finally started to feel accepted here, and we have even been allowed to visit Billy and Tom.

Ann is still nervous around her uncle, and having met him, we can understand why. But, we keep thinking back to the time when Ann said that she thought her uncle might be feeling scared too. The first time we met Tom, he was still very poorly, but Eva and I were invited because we had helped to find him, and made it possible for him to be looked after until he can get well again. I can remember looking into his dark, sad, almost hollow eyes, and seeing what I thought was a longing to be able to turn back the clock, to a time before the last war and the horrors he had seen and suffered.

***

The long harsh winter was finally over, and spring was changing this little village every day. Blossoms were giving colour and life to hedgerows and trees, as well as gardens, baby animals and birds could be found everywhere. Our greatest treat is to be able to visit the farm and see the lambs and calves that are being born all the time. Even school was becoming quite fun, and although we still missed mother and home, we didn't cry so much now. We often still thought about father, but still there had been no more news about him. By now, it seems that even Eva has almost accepted that we are not going to see him again, although sometimes when a plane flies over head even I find myself thinking that could be father's plane. Also every time a letter comes through from mother, something stirs within both of us, igniting a hope that perhaps father has been found alive after all. But it never is, and the news from home is always the same. All the letters say the same thing, that more houses have been bombed and life at home is getting harder all the time. These letters do make us cry, and we are constantly fearful for the safety of our mother and grandparents.

This particular day, the sun has been

106

shining from early morning, and we are so enjoying the walk home from school, that we forget the time completely. When the three of us eventually walk through the door, Ann's mother is waiting for us. Immediately assuming we are in trouble for being late, we freeze in the hallway and wait to be admonished for our tardiness. But, after a few seconds of silence have passed without the expected telling off, we decide that perhaps she is waiting for us to explain why we are late.

'Please ma'am, we are sorry to be so late, but the spring sunshine is so beautiful, and we were enjoying it so much, that we didn't want our journey home to end.'

'Elizabeth is right mama; it is so beautiful that we just wanted to stay out there forever.'

'Of course you want to enjoy the spring weather girls and each other's company no doubt. There is nothing wrong with that, but now I need to speak to Elizabeth and Eva on their own for a little while Ann, so take yourself up to your room, and the girls will join you as soon as they can.'

'We don't mind Ann staying if she wants to, we will tell her everything anyway.'

'That will be your decision girls, but I really think that I should talk to you alone first, I have some exciting news from your mother which I am sure will please you.'

Will Eva's constant denial of our father's death really prove to be the right thing after all? She cannot wait to ask the question.

'Is it father? Has he been found alive at last? Is he coming home?'

'Slow down Eva; please do not get your hopes up falsely. Please come on in to the sitting room, and Ann can wait for you in the kitchen or in her room, it is her choice.'

'Don't worry Ann, we won't be long, we will come and find you in your room.'

'Alright, but please don't be too long.'

'Ann! Don't be so impatient! Eva and Elizabeth will join you as soon as they can. The longer you keep them talking now, the longer you will have to wait to hear their exciting news.'

Reluctantly Ann begins to climb the staircase and make her way to her room as Eva and I are gently ushered into the sitting room. The early evening sunshine of spring is sending dappled light across the floor and cushions on the settee, with the shadows of leaves and blossoms dancing in the playful breeze. Just being in this room fills us with a new sense of hope as we eagerly sit beside each other facing the window that looks out onto the pretty garden, awaiting the news contained within the small envelope held delicately in Ann's mother's slender ivory hand.

'Eva and Elizabeth, when you first came here you suffered a lot, and our aloofness and strict discipline did not help you feel secure and safe in any way. For this, I can only apologise and ask for your forgiveness. But now, we have you to thank for the bridges which are being built between our little family and my husband's surviving relatives, particularly his sister Joan. If you and Ann had listened to us and not gone out looking, we may never have found Tom in time, and now all three siblings are spending time together and getting to know each other properly. Tom still has his problems, and that may never change, but we have already noticed a change in him, and the kindness that you showed when you found him means everything to him and to the rest of us, especially Ann. I have not known her as happy as this for a very long while, so thank you for being such good friends to her.'

Eva and I sit listening, getting more and more anxious. What is Ann's mother trying to say? Are we to be sent somewhere else? Are they going somewhere else? What is happening here?

'Please don't look so worried girls, the news from your mother is good, but Eva, I'm afraid that it is not the news you are hoping for. I'm sorry child, I do so wish that I could tell you what you want to hear but I can't. However, what I am about to tell you will, I'm sure be very exciting for you both.

I received this letter from your mother this morning, and when I read its contents I just couldn't wait for you to get home from school. I know and understand how anxious you have both been about your mother and grandparents, but this letter tells you that they are now safe and will remain so. It also says that you will be able to be reunited with them all, much sooner than any of us could have ever imagined.'

'What do you mean ma'am? Has the bombing in London finally stopped? Are we going home?'

'Hush now girls, you will indeed be going home soon, but not back to London. The bombing there is still very bad, so your family have made the decision to move up to the far north of the country. At the moment they are all staying with your aunt and uncle, but they are looking for a small cottage that you and your mother will be able to call home. As soon as your mother is settled she will write again and all the necessary arrangements will be made to enable you both to join her. It will be a new start for all of you and I cannot tell you how pleased I am that you have got this opportunity.'

'But we will have to start all over again;

110

we won't have any friends because they will all be in London or here. Why can't we stay here and then go back to London when the bombing has finished?'

'We would love you to stay here, but your mother really does want you back and without your father she is not feeling settled in London anymore. You are all she has got left at the moment and you need to be with her. You will make new friends up there as easily as you have down here, it will be fun, and I understand that you have got cousins up there who are already really excited and cannot wait to get to know you.'

'We are going to miss Ann and Billy so much, when do we have to go?'

'I don't know that as yet, but as I understand it, it won't be until your mother has a place of her own, as it is her desire that you go straight to your new home.'

Both Eva and I sit in silence for several minutes trying to take in all that we have been told.

'Are you girls alright?'

'Please, may we go and see Ann now? We need to tell her our news, and as we will be leaving soon we want to spend as much time with her and Billy as possible.'

'Of course you may, but please try and look forward to this as a new adventure, not as something to be feared. Your mother would want you to be looking forward to being back with her, not fearing being in a new place. So you have both got to try to be as brave as you were when you came here alright?'

'We will try, and we really do want to see mother again, it is just that we wish father would be there with us too.'

'I know, it will be hard for all of you, but this is why your mother needs you with her now more than ever. Now run along before Ann comes down here looking for you.'

Eva and I leave the pretty sun-bathed sitting room, still feeling more than a little uncertain about all that we have just heard, and begin to climb the staircase. Before we can get even halfway up Ann is at the top waiting for us.

'You have been ages, what is happening? You don't look very happy; I thought you were getting good news, what is wrong?'

'You are not going to like it either when we tell you what we have just heard?'

'What do you mean? You are not going to leave here are you?'

Eva and I say nothing, but the look that passes between us is enough for Ann to start jumping to the right conclusions.

'You can't go away now, you can't! I

won't let you! I have always been so lonely, but when you arrived here everything changed, even father is kinder now. I have never known what true friendship felt like; you are the only real friends I have got now, so you can't leave me so soon.'

'Ann, please believe us when we tell you that we don't want to go, but our mother wants us back with her. We are not even going back to our house in London, we are being forced to move to another new place, and what makes it worse is that father won't even be there.'

'It's not fair; I hoped you would stay here forever.'

'That was never going to happen Ann; we were always going to return home to our parents eventually, you know that. Besides when we first came here you didn't even want us here.'

'That was because of father, I didn't want to be like that. I guess I always knew deep down that you would have to go back, but not so soon. This horrible war isn't even over yet.'

I make no reply, but turn my attention instead to the letter which Ann's mother has given us so that we can read its contents for ourselves. I do this more to hide my own feelings than for any other reason. I take the letter out of the envelope and begin to read;

only stopping when Ann's voice breaks through the tense silence.

'Elizabeth, what does the letter say? When have you got to leave?'

'Even we don't know that yet Ann, but I can tell you what the letter says if you would like me too?'

'I haven't seen the letter yet Elizabeth! Can I see it first, before you share it with anyone else?'

Eva's tone is so sharp that Ann looks as if she is going to cry.

'Eva, that was not kind. Ann is our friend, and the letter doesn't say anything we don't already know.'

'I'm sorry Ann, I didn't mean to be nasty, it is just that I don't quite believe what is happening myself. Do you want to read it for yourself Ann?'

'I don't know, I don't really like the thought of reading other people's letters, can you just tell me what it says?'

'Alright, but it doesn't answer all our questions, so I know it won't answer all yours. Our mother and grandparents have left London after their house was destroyed by a bomb. They have moved up to the north, deep in the countryside. They say it is safer up there; our mother is going to send for us as soon as she is settled in a place of her own, instead of living with our aunt, uncle, cousins and grandparents. We will be together again, but without our dear father, so I don't think it will ever really feel like home. Our lives are being turned upside down yet again, and now you and Billy are going to suffer too. This is all so wrong.'

By now none of us can speak as we are all in tears and unable to stop, we don't even hear when Ann's mother calls us for tea. It is only when Ann's mother appears in the doorway of Ann's room and tells us that tea is on the table that we realise how long we have been up here.

'Oh goodness girls, whatever is the matter? Surely such great distress is not due to that letter from your mother is it? The news it contains is meant to bring joy not heartache.'

'Oh but mama, it's not fair, why do Elizabeth and Eva have to leave just when we are becoming really good friends?'

'Now Ann, listen to me, I am sure that the girls have already told you that they don't know when they are leaving yet, so instead of crying and letting your tea get cold, you need to start enjoying their company and planning your next adventure with them. I am sure you will have many more before they have to leave. Elizabeth and Eva want to enjoy their remaining time here, don't you girls?'

'We do, but not knowing how long we
115

are to remain here means there is such a heavy shadow hanging over us, that it feels as if it is going to stop us from having any fun.'

To our great surprise, and not a little dismay, Ann's mother starts to giggle and shake her head.

'Please ma'am, can you tell us what it is that we said that you find so amusing?'

'Oh I'm sorry girls, you make this news from your mother sound so melodramatic, you know you will always have Ann's friendship. She can write to you, and you can write to her, who knows, we might even be able to arrange a visit or two in the holidays.'

'Oh mama, do you really mean it?'

'Ann, you know I don't say things I don't mean, but right at this minute your father is waiting.'

The news of possible visits seems to lift us all from our pit of despondency, and we suddenly realise what Ann's mother had said to us when she first entered the room.

'Please ma'am; did you say we were to come downstairs for tea too? Or were you just talking to Ann?'

'Yes girls, you are to join us for all your meals from now on, we should never have made you eat alone in the first place. Besides, tonight's tea is special and it is my husband who has requested that you join us. Tom is finally well enough to come back home, and

116

John would like us to all to eat together to celebrate.'

Ann's face changes, and the look in her eyes is one of anxiety and fear once more. This time it is Eva who sees it first.

'Ann, what's wrong? Are you still nervous about your uncle?'

She nods meekly and looks to her mother for comfort and reassurance.

'It's alright Ann, your uncle is not a dangerous man, he poses no threat to you, he never has. It is just that sometimes he has bad thoughts and they frighten him, a bit like you girls sometimes have a bad dream. Anyway, I know that Tom has got something he wishes to say to all of you.'

Eva and I both gasp, and try to disguise the fear we are also beginning to feel.

'Why are you two looking so startled? You both played your part in helping Tom too; Ann couldn't have done it alone. It is only natural that he would wish to meet and thank you properly.

Now if we stay up here any longer the tea will be spoiled, so dry your eyes, tidy yourselves up and I will see you down there in a few minutes.'

Ann's mother leaves the room and the three of us just stare at each other before trying to make ourselves look presentable. Just as Ann, Eva and I are about to leave the

117

room, Ann stops and returns to her small white-painted dressing table. Opening one of the small drawers, she removes something without us being able to see what it is.

'Elizabeth, Eva, before we go down, I want you to have these back so that you too can wear your hair flowing and pretty as it should be. Open yours hands please.'

We look at each other bemused, what is she talking about? But we hold out our hands, as by now we are getting hungry, and we really don't want to upset Ann's father now he seems to be finally beginning to accept us.

She opens each of her hands over ours and drops the contents of each fist onto our waiting palms.

'I have kept these safe for you. They have never been used in my hair as they were not mine to begin with.'

As we glance down at our hands we can hardly believe our eyes.

'Oh Ann, are they really our ribbons? The ones we were sent from mother at Christmas time?'

'They are! Here, let me put them in for you.'

Eva and I are so shocked, we allow Ann to tie them into our hair, as we don't want to seem ungrateful. Although deep down we are dreading what her father will say when he sees them.

'There, that is much better, now we look more like sisters than friends.'

Ann seems almost triumphant about the whole thing, as though she is teaching her father a lesson. Eva and I both know that this could be a very dangerous game to play. Nevertheless, we finally leave Ann's room and make our way down the main staircase to join in a family meal for the first time since we arrived.

To our surprise, and great relief, Ann's father does not mention the hair ribbons at all, and welcomes us to the table with almost a smile on his usually stern, hard-featured face. Tom is sitting beside him, looking almost as nervous as we are. Before we start to eat Ann's father stands to say grace. This brings a lump to my throat, and when I look at Eva, her eyes are closed more tightly than is necessary. For both of us, this simple act reminds us so much of mealtimes at home before the war. Father always said grace before we ate, and until now, we had not experienced this for many months. Will our own dear father ever do this for us again? I hear a sniff from beside me and know that the same thought has just crossed the mind of my twin.

The food is delicious, and despite the news of our impending departure, we eat and drink much more than we have for a long while. At the end of the meal, Tom is the one who shakily stands up to speak, and I can sense Ann tighten on the other side of me.

'I am extremely thankful to finally be well enough to return home. I am fully aware how much anguish and heartache I have caused my brother and his family, not just over recent weeks, but over many years. I can only apologise for this, and promise to try at least, to be a better houseguest, uncle, brother and brother-in-law in the years to come.'

My eyes are drawn in the direction of Ann's father, and it is obvious that he is feeling overcome, and he has bowed his head to conceal his true feelings. Tom is obviously still very weak, and almost collapses back onto his chair, but steadying himself once more; he takes a deep breath and continues.

'I am also aware that for several years, my own niece has been afraid of me, and yet it is to her, and her two new friends, Elizabeth and Eva, that I now owe my life. I am most grateful to all three of you. The courage and care you have shown me is immensely humbling, and Elizabeth and Eva, I fully intend to write to your parents telling them how proud they can be of both of you. Thank you Ann, thank you Elizabeth and thank you Eva.'

With every ounce of energy exhausted, Tom finally falls back on to his seat at the table breathing heavily.

I glance at Eva and can see that she is blushing, and I can feel heat rising up my neck and face, so I know I too am blushing. I can also feel tears, hot and salty, waiting to fall, but manage to swallow hard and prevent their escape, at least for now.

For several minutes there is silence around the table, not a sad, solemn silence, but a silence of gratitude and hope. Then, it is Ann's father who gives Ann, Eva and I permission to leave the table, suggesting that perhaps we would like to take a walk in the garden before we go to bed. This invitation is one all three of us accept enthusiastically as the sun is resting on the horizon, filling the gardens with its warm, orange glow.

The cool evening air is both refreshing and calming and all three of us just sit on the small bench and enjoy the fragranced-filled tranquillity that is so evident here. Then, Eva breaks this restful quietness with a question we have all been avoiding.

'When are we going to tell Billy about leaving? Do you think he will still want to be friends with us?'
Unable to find any answers to my sister's questions, I just look at her, and then at Ann before trying to change the subject.

'The sun has all but gone now, and it is getting chilly, perhaps we should go back indoors now?'

I get up from the bench and begin to move towards the door. But Ann is the one who stops me in my tracks and Eva from shouting at me.

'Well, you have told me and I still want to be your friend, so I can't see why Billy won't want to be. I think we should all tell him together after school tomorrow, and then it is up to him. The sooner he knows the better, or he might guess that you are keeping something from him, and that isn't fair.'
With that, Ann also gets up and moves across the garden to join me. Eva, unable to argue with Ann's common sense suggestion, also gets up and eventually joins us beneath a beautiful flowering cherry tree.

'It is a bit chilly out here now, and I'm feeling a bit tired, even if you're not.'

She seems to be getting more and more determined to have the last word, but I don't want an argument, so Ann and I follow her in and make our way to the staircase. Before we can even begin climbing the stairs, the door of the pretty sitting room opens, and Ann's father appears.

'Elizabeth and Eva, could you come in here for just a moment please?'
Looking nervously at each other we duly obey, wondering what we have done wrong now.

'Please don't look so anxious girls, I know that I have not made your time here particularly easy, and for that I can only apologise. I freely admit that I was worried about strangers coming into my home, and the effect it would have on my family. I can see now that your presence here has only brought joy where there had been none for a long time, and for this I thank you. Ann is a different child since you arrived, and I know that she will miss you more than anyone when you have to leave. But this is not why I have asked you in here tonight.

I know how tired you must be, you have had a lot to take in today, but I wanted to say that from now on you will eat all your meals with us, and for however long or short your remaining time here might be, from tomorrow you will move down out of the attic and into the room next to Ann's towards the back of the house which is overlooking the garden. However, I do expect you to sleep and not creep in and out of each other's rooms, do you understand?'

'Oh yes, we promise, and thank you for all you have done for us. We have not meant to cause you any trouble, but mother has always told us that if we thought we could help somebody then we should always try. That is all we have tried to do sir.'

'I know, and for that we are all most

grateful, and from now on you may refer to us as Mr John and Mrs Agnes, it is less formal than sir or ma'am. Now, off to bed, and tomorrow while you are at school, we will ensure that your belongings are moved to your new room. Good night and God bless both of you.'

We leave the room having wished them the same, only to find Ann sitting on the stairs waiting for us, and looking close to tears.

'Did you get into trouble about the hair ribbons? It is all my fault; I should have just given them to you instead of insisting that you wear them. I am so sorry; I will go in and explain now.'

'Oh Ann, there is no need, we are not in trouble at all, but we will all be if we don't go up to bed!'

As the three of us climb the stairs, Eva and I explain to Ann exactly what did happen in the sitting room.

'Your father never even mentioned the hair ribbons, he is so different now.'

As we say goodnight to Ann outside her room, and then make our way up to the little attic for the last time, we know we will sleep tonight.

Sure enough the next time we open our eyes, the birds are singing and the spring sunshine is glistening through the tiny window. Although we are glad to be leaving this draughty, sparsely furnished, almost forgotten little room, something about it is almost calling to us to remember it and not ignore it completely. But the excitement of being down in the main house is so overwhelming, that this feeling is soon forgotten.

When we are ready, we make our way down towards Ann's room and then to breakfast. But before we get to the kitchen where breakfast is eaten, Eva and I suddenly remember what we have got to do when school finishes today. We have got to tell Billy that we will be leaving soon. Our appetite seems to disappear, and by the time we are seated, the very thought of food makes us feel almost sick. Ann looks at us anxiously as if she knows exactly what is going through our heads. Our plate is filled with toast, an egg and half a piece of bacon. It looks delicious and an egg is a real treat for us, it has come from Billy's farm, but our ability to eat any of it still seems unlikely.

'Ann, Elizabeth, Eva, you may start, we don't want you to be late for school, and Tom needs to rest this morning so we shall eat with him later.'

'Thank you ma'am... I mean Mrs Agnes.'

Eva and I pick up our toast and begin nibbling at one corner, thinking that if we are late for school it might be a good thing this morning. We would be kept back at lunchtime and Billy would be gone before we could say anything. Surprisingly, as we eat a little our appetite returns and soon there are three empty plates on the kitchen table.

'Now, run along and remember, when you come home you will be in your new room.'

The last part of this remark from Ann's mother is meant for me and Eva, but Ann seems more excited than we are. It is almost as if she is moving too.

The journey to school is beautiful in the sunshine, just as yesterday's had been, but the knowledge that we have to tell Billy our news seems to be stealing much of our enjoyment and pleasure. We arrive at the school gates just as Billy does, and something inside me wants to blurt it out now to get it over with, but the bell for school to start is already ringing, so it will have to wait until afterwards.

Most of the time these mornings in school seem to last forever, but today it just feels as if it is racing by too fast. Before we know it lunchtime is here and so is the time for us to tell Billy. As usual, Billy cannot wait to be free so he is first to leave the classroom. Eva and I take our time, hoping that he will have gone before we get out to the gate.

'Come on you two, Billy is waiting to show us some new ducklings on the pond at the farm.'

This is going to make telling him even harder, but the chance to see some baby ducklings is too great to resist.

'Alright Ann, we're coming'

'You're not still worried about telling him that you're leaving soon are you? He will be fine, I know it. I wish I was coming too, they have mountains in the north, father told me. Just think how exciting that will be. I can't wait until I can come and visit.'

By the time we reach the gate, Billy is getting fidgety.

'Where have you been? You coming to the pond today or not?'

'Of course we are coming Billy, but Eva and Elizabeth have got some news of their own to tell you first.'

'Well, what is it? Bet it's not as exciting as baby ducklings! Girls news never is.'

'Oh yes it is! Go on tell him!'

Eva and I just stand and look at each other before I take a deep breath and take the letter from mother out of my pocket. Sliding it carefully out of the envelope, I am just about to start reading it to Billy, when the playful spring breeze snatches it from my hand.

'Oh no, that letter is from our mother, please help us catch it.'

Billy is already chasing it before I even finish talking, and by the time we catch up with him, he has already started reading it for himself. When he has finished he hands it back to me and says nothing.

'Are you alright Billy? Aren't you going to say anything? We were just about to tell you, please don't be cross. It is not our fault, we don't want to go but our mother needs us.'

I stop, this is the first time I have realised for myself that mother is alone and frightened too.

'I'm not cross, I'm jealous, and what can I say? It must be so exciting to be going somewhere new. I'll never get to see nowhere different like that.'

'You don't know that Billy. Maybe you can come and visit us with Ann?'

'Eva's right, Ann is going to come in the holidays, you could come with her.'

'Do you think your pa would let me Ann? He has only just let us be friends.'

'I'm sure he would, now can we go and see the ducklings?'

With Billy's frown turning back to his usual cheeky grin, he agrees and we run the rest of the way to the farm.

'Now you'll have to be quiet or you'll scare them.'

Billy carefully parts the long grass at the

128

side of the pond, and there, dabbling at the water's edge are six tiny fluffy ducklings. We stay watching them for several minutes before Billy's mother appears at the other side of the pond. Her voice is little more than a whisper, but Billy knows not to argue.

'Billy, leave them poor little things be, you're enough like a fairy elephant to scare them to death!'

'Sorry ma, I just wanted the girls to see them.'

'Alright, you lot better all come in and have a drink before you go.'

'Yes please, can we have another look before we go?'

'We'll see, now come on into the house.'

The four of us all follow Billy's mother into the farmhouse and take a seat at the table in the kitchen. A large glass of milk is put down in front of each of us. The creamy liquid is delicious and all the glasses are very soon emptied.

Ma, Eva and Elizabeth are going away soon, and they said that in the holidays I can go and see them, can I ma, can I, please?'

Oh Billy, we'll have to see, but you know your pa needs help on the farm, so it will depend when it is. Where are you off to my dears, back to London?'

'Nah, not London ma, they're going up

to the north.'

'I wasn't asking you Billy Elder, let them speak for themselves.'

'Billy is right Mrs Elder, London is still being badly bombed so it is too dangerous, and besides, our mother wants us all to have a new start. We don't really want to go. We have made friends here now and we won't know anyone up there but mother needs us. She is missing father dreadfully like we are, so we have to go for her.'

'I see, well don't you go worrying about not having any friends, you'll soon make new ones just like you have down here. Two friendly, kind-hearted little lasses like you, you'll fit right in wherever you go.

Well now, another visit to the ducklings before you and Ann go home?'

'Yes please, if that is alright?'

'Billy, you can take them, but just go quietly and don't get too close or the mother will get upset and may even abandon her babies.'

'Alright ma.'

This time we creep towards the pond, and now when Billy parts the grass, the mother duck is back on the nest and the babies are nowhere to be seen.

'She's brooding them; they are underneath her to keep warm. Look, there's one sticking his head out. Come on we better leave them now or ma will be after me.'

Leaving the ducks in peace and the pond behind us, Billy walks with us until we reach the road.

'Come back and see them again soon, they grow really fast.'

'We will, and thank you for showing them to us Billy they are really sweet.'
We don't speak much on the way back to Ann's, and despite the enjoyable walk we are quicker than yesterday as Eva and I are eager to see our new room.

When we arrive back at Ann's house, once again Ann's mother is there to greet us, only this time, instead of her usual smile; we can see by her face that something is wrong. Ann also notices, and from the look on her face she may already know what is happening, or at the very least suspect something.

'Mama, what is wrong? Is it Tom? Has something happened? Please mama tell me what it is?'

'All in good time Ann, first we must show Elizabeth and Eva their new room. It is all prepared for you girls, we managed to do that before... Oh never mind, if you would like to follow me I will take you there now. I am sure you are excited to see it aren't you?'

'Oh yes Mrs Agnes, but if you need to speak to Ann, I am sure we can find our own way.'

'Thank you for your concern girls, but I am afraid that what I have to say concerns all of you, so it is better that we get you settled first.'

Ann looks at us, and we look at her, what can be so awful? We know it must be awful because of the look on Ann's mother's face and the almost hollow sound to her voice, but why does it involve us? We are not even part of the family, and if it is about our father, then why does it involve Ann? Nothing seems to be making any sense!

We follow Ann's mother in silence up to our new room, and there seems to be a solemn stillness and silence throughout the house reflecting what is now, our own sombre mood. However, when we reach our new room and the door is opened we are overwhelmed and our spirits are instantly lifted. This pretty little room is flooded with the afternoon sunshine, and the room is almost a mirror image of Ann's.

'Oh, oh Mrs Agnes, this is beautiful, we will be very happy in here, thank you, thank you, thank you. We never thought that we would have our own beds too, this is just like a fairytale.'

'I am so glad you like it girls, and I am glad it has made you so happy, but when you have arranged it as you want it, I must ask you all to join me in the sitting room, as what

I have to say is serious. It will mean a great deal of changes for all of us.'

Without waiting for a reply, Ann's mother turns and leaves the three of us staring at each other. For once, none of us can think of anything to say. We get to work organising our few belongings in and around the room, this does not take long as we do not have much to organize, but our photograph of father has pride of place in the centre of the small ivory dressing table. We do not linger for long, as something in what Ann's mother said makes us believe that the news we are about to hear is not just awful, but urgent. So, closing the door of our new room behind us, we make our way downstairs to the sitting room.

Unusually the door is already open, so the three of us enter nervously and huddle together on the settee opposite Ann's mother and await the news with a growing sense of dread.

'Oh girls, there is no easy way to tell you what I must, but it is also not fair to keep it from you. In fact, it will soon be impossible. I have asked all three of you to be here because I am afraid that Elizabeth and Eva will have to leave us as soon as the arrangements can be made. I have already written to their mother explaining the situation, and the letter was posted earlier this afternoon. I know this is unexpected girls, but please do not think that you are no longer wanted here, because nothing could be further from the truth.'

Ann grabs both our hands tightly and will not let them go.

'But surely our dear mother has not written again already saying that she has found a house? We only got her other letter yesterday.'

'Oh Eva, I truly wish that were the case, but I am afraid that it is not your mother who needs you to leave urgently, but me.'

Ann's mother pauses, struggling to stay in control of her own feelings, her voice becoming thick and croaky with emotion.

'But why mama? What is going on?'

Then, with a look of real horror on her face, Ann continues.

'Where is papa? Why isn't he here? If the news you have to share is that important, then he should be here too!'

Unable to hide her feelings any longer, Ann's mother pulls her chair towards the settee so she can be closer to us, places her hands over the top of her daughters so that she has got contact with all three of us.

'Oh my dear Ann, if your father could be here he would be my darling, but that is part of what I am finding so hard to tell you. Your father only told me this morning, after you had gone to school.'

'Told you what mama? Where is he? Why can't he be here?'

'Please Ann let me finish, it is hard enough for me to say without you continually interrupting me. About three weeks ago your father received a letter which I did not know about myself until this morning. This letter was official, and contained his military call up papers. This morning he had to leave to take up his commission in the Army. He felt it was better for him to leave before you got home, so that you wouldn't have to see him go. I pleaded with him saying that you would want to say goodbye, but his mind was made up. He did however write you a letter for me to give to you when I had explained everything.'

'Oh mama, please may I have it now, I want to read it with my friends beside me.'

'Oh Ann please be patient for just a little longer, I am afraid I still haven't finished. If it were just your father's absence, then Elizabeth and Eva could stay, in fact I would be glad for them too, but there is something else I have to tell you. Your father and I were going to wait to tell you this, but his sudden departure means that you need to know.'

'Know what mama?'

Ann's voice is little more than a whisper now

because she too has been crying so much.

'Well, I am hoping that this news might cheer you up a little, I am expecting a baby. You are going to have a baby brother or sister. But this does mean that when the time comes for me to have the baby, I am going to need some help here at home. So, with your father's agreement, you will finally get to know your grandparents. They have agreed to move in here while your father is away and they cannot wait to meet you, but it is not fair to expect them to look after three lively girls, which is why I am afraid, Eva and Elizabeth are going to have to leave as soon as their mother can arrange things. You do understand don't you girls?'

'Of course, thank you for telling us, we will be ready to go when we have to Mrs Agnes.'

'Mama, do you think I could have my letter from papa now?'

'Of course child, I will leave you three girls alone so that you can share it with your friends.'

Handing Ann a small white envelope, her mother gets up from her chair and begins to walk towards the door.

'Mama, please stay, I don't want you to leave. I want us all to stay together until Elizabeth and Eva have to leave, I'm scared. What if my grandparents don't like me?

136

Can't I go and stay on the farm with Billy instead?'

'Oh my darling, of course your grandparents will like you, and besides, I know that you will want to meet your new brother or sister when they arrive won't you? Then, you will be able to write to Elizabeth and Eva telling them all your exciting news, and they will be able to tell you theirs.'

'Mama, is papa going to be flying a plane like Elizabeth and Eva's father is?'

'No darling, their father is in the Royal Air Force; your father is in the Army.'

'So what does that mean? Will he have to use a gun and see things like Uncle Tom had to?'

Ann's mother pauses, gulps, swallows hard and takes several deep breaths before answering Ann again.

'He will almost certainly have to carry a weapon, and yes, he may well see some horrible things darling, but he will always know that we are waiting for him to return home. We will pray for him every day, and whatever the distances between us, he will always know that we love him very much.'

'But mama, how will he know?'

'Well, you know that he loves you, even when you are at school don't you?'

'Yes mama, of course I do, and he tells me every night when I come home. Oh

137

mama, he won't be able to do that now will he?'

'Hush Ann, he will be able to feel our love in the same way we can feel his, and although he may not be here, there is nothing to stop you telling him how much you love him every night if it helps you to say it out loud. I am sure he will be saying it to you wherever he is, and he has promised to write as often as he can.'

Eva and I have sat in silence throughout until now, but we know just how Ann is feeling and want to help, we just don't really know how to.

'Ann, Eva and I both know how horrible this feels, and it will always feel strange and difficult until he comes home, but your mother needs you more than ever now.'

'I know, and it must be even worse for you because you don't even know if your father is still alive, and when you leave, you are not even going home. I just wish this stupid war was over.'

'I think that is what we all want darling. Now, how about some tea and then maybe we can all go out for a walk this evening. I think it might help us all to sleep a little better after such a difficult day, and the weather is so beautiful, it is a shame not to enjoy it.'

We all reluctantly agree, though none of us

feel hungry, and we don't really believe her either. Sleep is not going to come easily to any of us tonight.

Part 4

Ann's father has only been gone a few days, but the house is already a very different place, and in spite of the way he treated us when we first arrived here, even we find ourselves missing him. But, the person who is struggling to adapt to John's absence the most is his brother Tom. He often just sits in the garden and rocks to and fro as if he is trying to ease a pain. Even when we ask him if he is alright, he just keeps telling us that hearing us in the house is a comfort to him. But we don't really know what he means, and he never seems to be comforted. Ann's mother says it is because he had believed the last war was supposed to bring an end to conflicts, and he feels betrayed because it didn't. She also thinks he feels guilty because he has not been able to prevent his younger brother from having to face what he has already been through.

'But Mrs Agnes, none of that is not Tom's fault, he didn't start this war. Why should he blame himself?'

'I cannot answer that question girls, but even if I could, I do not think that it would change his way of thinking I'm afraid.'

141

Knowing that Tom is blaming himself is really hard, and Ann is missing her father dreadfully. Seeing her like this is only increasing our own feelings of separation and fear for our own dear father. But so far there has been no news from our mother, so at least our departure is not imminent yet. Billy is still being a really good friend to all three of us, but that is just making the thought of our leaving even harder to cope with. However, at least we know Ann will not be alone when we do have to go. Many of the friends who left London with us, have either gone home already because their parents were missing them too much, or they have moved to other places where they had other relatives. Somehow, this only makes our move even harder to bear, because we will not be able to see them at all where we are going.

***

Just a few short weeks ago we had finally started to settle in and feel secure here, and very soon now we are going to have to start all over again. We are walking home from school this afternoon, and the weather is just getting better and better, but something feels different. There is an uneasiness that seems to be hanging over me. Eva seems to be unaffected by it, but for me the nearer we get to Ann's house, the more intense it seems to get.

142

Ann is the first to notice, and before she says anything, she takes hold of my hand and grips it tightly in her own.

'Are you alright Elizabeth? You are really quiet this afternoon. Do you feel unwell?'

'I don't really know what is wrong Ann, it is just a strange feeling I have got! I don't mean to be so quiet, and I am not ill, I just feel uneasy, as if something is going to happen.'

It is only now that Eva looks at me, and I can see that despite her being as chatty as normal, she too is feeling something.

'Are you feeling it too Elizabeth? Do you think that our time to leave has arrived?'

It is only now she has put her feelings into words that I understand my own. That question is the one I had not wanted to put into words.

'I fear you may be right Eva, but we must be brave, our mother needs us and would not want us to fear this.'

Eva nods, and the rest of our journey home is a quiet and thoughtful one.

When we arrive and enter the house, we cannot find Ann's mother anywhere, and begin to doubt our feelings. But we eventually find her sitting with Tom in the pretty back garden.

'Oh hello girls, have you not been to

the farm today?'

'No Mrs Agnes, Billy did ask us to go, but something inside me was telling me we needed to come straight home. Ann and Eva did not seem to want to go either.'

'I see, you must have guessed that a letter from your mother arrived this morning. The arrangements for you to join her have all been made. It is indeed time for you to go, and we will all miss you very much. You have been a great comfort to both Tom and me, but most of all a true friend to Ann, thank you.'

'Please Mrs Agnes, how soon do we have to leave?'

Having gone back into the pretty sitting room, Ann's mother takes the letter down from its resting place on the mantle piece and removes it carefully from the envelope.

'The arrangements are all now in place and you are to travel by train on Monday next week as far as Penrith station. Someone will meet you when you leave the train there and take you to your Aunt and Uncle's house where you will be reunited with your mother. Ann and I will accompany you to the station and see you safely on the train here, so there is no need to fear.'

'Monday is only three days away, so that means today was our last day at school here wasn't it? We have to see Billy tomorrow; you will let us go to the farm won't you? It will be our last chance! Oh why does it have to be so soon?'

'After how unhappy you were during your first few months here, I would have thought that you would be glad to leave by now, but you still seem to be reluctant? I know you are worried about making new friends, but whenever you go that will be the same, and the sooner you go the sooner those friendships can start to grow. Do you see?'

'Oh Mrs Agnes, we do see, but what if no-one wants to be friends with us?'

'Can you remember your first day at school here, when Billy wanted to be your friend straightaway? Well then, why should it be any different up in the north in your new school?'

'It shouldn't, but what about our teacher here, doesn't she need to know that we will not be going back?'

'That has already been taken care of; do you remember the lady at the church hall who let us bring you home when you first arrived? Well she has a special job to do. She is called a billeting officer, which means she is responsible for housing all evacuees while they are here and sorting out any problems for you. So, I have been to see her as she has to be told when you are moving on, and she has told your teacher.

As for Billy, of course you can see him tomorrow, why don't you bring him back here for tea? Then we can have a proper little farewell party for you.'

'Oh Mrs Agnes, can we really? Thank you, thank you so much, thank you for everything.'

'That is quite alright girls. Now why don't you and Ann go out into the garden and enjoy this beautiful afternoon?'

'Can I please show them the secret place mama? I really would like them to see it before they go away.'

'Of course you can darling, just be careful not to disturb anything that might be living there alright?'

'Yes mama.'

Ann practically bounces off the settee, and we can barely keep up with her. What is she so excited about? We have been in the garden before, especially recently, we know how beautiful it is, but until now, Ann has barely even seemed to notice. This sudden change in her is quite out of character and must mean there is something really exciting to see, but where? The garden is surrounded on all sides by high walls covered in either climbing roses, which are covered in prickles, or thick dark leaved creepers which always look as if they are about to swallow up anyone who goes near them. The only gate appears to be the one we escaped through when we crept out to search for Tom.

'Ann, wait! Why are you in such a hurry? We have got all afternoon, and we have seen the garden many times already.'

'Not all of it, this place is special.'

'But Ann, the garden is surrounded by walls, how do we get there? Do we have to go through the gate?'

'Wait and see!'

Her reply is so gleefully delivered, that it sounds almost as if she is laughing, it is certainly obvious that she is taking great delight in keeping this secret from us for as long as possible.

By now we are in the garden and standing in front of one of the walls which is covered in a huge creeper. It is only now that we are this close to it that we realise that the most beautiful, delicate blossoms in the whole garden are attached to this mysterious tree. We are longing to ask Ann what it is called, but there is no time as she is already sliding in behind it, and we are afraid of losing sight of her if we don't follow her immediately. However, we follow reluctantly convinced that we will just end up trapped against a cold, slimy, damp wall, and then not be able to get out. We could not have been more wrong! By the time Eva and I have also squeezed behind the creeper with the lovely flowers, we find ourselves standing, not against a horrible, dirty wall, but in a very much smaller, but equally as beautiful second garden.

'Oh Ann, what is this place? Why is it kept so hidden?'
Ann's face is glowing with satisfaction and delight, in the certain knowledge that she managed to tempt us into following her here without telling us anything!

'This is our secret place, known only to mama and me. Mama discovered it one day while she was here alone, in the early days before me, and after her parents had stopped visiting because of papa. She has been coming here every day since, even in the winter! I only found it because I followed her one day like you have just followed me. Isn't it just lovely?'

'It is perfect, but how can you be certain that your father doesn't know about it?'

'Well, he has never talked about it, and mama has always asked me not to tell him, saying that it would always be our own little secret place. Somewhere we could come if we were sad or wanted to be alone. But now you have seen it too, you must never tell anyone, not even Billy. Do you promise?'

Very reluctantly we agree, but only after Ann agrees to us coming back here again before we have to leave. It would be very easy to forget the time in a place like this, but the gentle voice of Ann's mother can be faintly heard from the other side of the creeper-covered wall calling us in for tea.

Neither Eva nor I feel very hungry, our rapidly approaching departure seems to be almost stifling us, and yet this new special place seems to be almost telling us that everything will be alright. Even as we leave it for today, the new comfort we have found since we entered it stays with us. In fact, so much so that as we are climbing into bed tonight, having eaten much more than we thought we would, it is as if we can still smell the wonderful perfume that hung on the breeze there.

Unfortunately, we wake up this morning to the sound of rain dripping and trickling down the window. The sky has lost its lovely spring blueness and is now a sort of dirty white colour.

'Oh why does it have to rain today? We are supposed to visit Billy and invite him back here for tea. Now we are going to have to leave without saying goodbye. It's not fair.'

'Eva, don't be silly, just because it is raining doesn't mean we can't see Billy, or invite him back here for tea. It just means that...'

'Means what Elizabeth?'

'Oh nothing, it doesn't matter. We better go down for breakfast though or we won't be going anywhere.'

We leave our room just as Ann is leaving her room, so the three of us make our way downstairs together. We arrive at the kitchen, but something is wrong. Ann's mother is sitting with her arms resting on the table and her head buried in her hands. She is crying, and there is no sign of Tom.

'Mrs Agnes, are you alright? Please, have we upset you?'

'Oh girls, I'm sorry I didn't even hear you come in. Let me see about getting you some breakfast.'

She rises more slowly than usual from the table, and begins to cook some eggs and toast.

'Mama what is wrong? Is it papa? What has happened? Why are you so sad? Has Uncle Tom gone away again?'

'Ann! Please do not ask anymore, when I can tell you I will. Now, fill the kettle for me and put it on the stove, there's a good girl.'

Eva and I remain silent, but can feel the tension and know that something really bad must have happened.

Breakfast is eaten with very little conversation passing between any of us. Then, as the plates are being cleared, it is Eva who summons up her courage.

'Please Mrs Agnes, can we help? Don't be sad, we don't really mind leaving. Our mother needs us and we know that you will have enough to do without us soon.'

'Oh Eva, thank you. Both you and Elizabeth are such thoughtful girls. I am not sad because you are leaving, although I will miss you, there is another reason for my sadness this morning.'

She stops what she is doing and looks out of the window at the rain, before turning round to look at all of us. She takes a deep breath, wipes her eyes again, and tries to put on her smile, without much success.

'This is supposed to be a day of celebration, and I'm afraid this rain is not going to help. Nevertheless, a party is what I promised you, and a party is what we shall have. Now you girls would like Billy to come wouldn't you?'

'Yes please Mrs Agnes, but how can we go to the farm to collect him without getting wet?'

'Perhaps the rain will stop later so that you don't have to get wet.'

'Do you really think it will? It doesn't look much like it at the moment.'

Eva's obvious disgust at the weather even causes Ann's mother to smile, and for the first time this morning the heaviness that has surrounded us seems to lift a little.

With the knowledge that we need to be ready to leave here for good early on Monday morning, we spend this morning collecting as many of our belongings together as we can and putting them into the two small battered suitcases we had brought from home. Only when we open them do we find the last letters we received from father before we left London. Even without reading them our eyes become blurry and start to sting, so we hurriedly start putting other things on top of them. However, we already know that our thoughts today are all going to be influenced by him and it is only now that we know they always will be.

Packing our things will not take long, but we know it needs doing, and Ann's mother needs time alone with her daughter. We are desperate to know what terrible misfortune has occurred, but are very aware that it is not our business. Mother would be furious if she thought we had ever asked such a question, though we still hope Ann might tell us at least something about it later on.

We have also decided to write Ann and her mother a letter each that they can open when we have gone. We know how hard Monday is going to be, and both feel that we can say things better this way. By the time we have finished doing these two things, our room looks almost as barren as the attic had been when we first arrived, but at least the rain has stopped.

'Come on Elizabeth, Ann must be ready to come to the farm with us now. If we hurry we might even get there before it rains again.'

'I don't think it is going to rain anymore Eva look, the sun is trying to shine now.'

'So, what are you waiting for? Come on or we will never get there.'

'Eva, I think perhaps we should leave Ann with her mother and go to the farm on our own today. Something tells me they need time together, and Billy is coming back here for tea this afternoon anyway.'

'I don't think Ann will like being left behind here, I know I wouldn't. Shouldn't we at least ask her if she wants to come with us?' Reluctantly I agree to call at the kitchen before we go. To our surprise the kitchen is empty, so we head towards the sitting room. The door is shut and we can just make out the voice of Ann's mother in the room beyond. Timidly we knock on the door and wait, for several seconds there is no response, and I am just about to tell Eva we should go, when the door opens.

'Hello girls, thank you for being so patient with us this morning. I have spoken to Ann and said that it is up to her to tell you as much or as little as she wants too. I know that you will not push her and respect this, as you have ever since you arrived. However, I think perhaps some fresh air would do us all good now that the rain has stopped, would you mind if I came to the farm with you today?'

'Not at all, we would love you to come.'

'I was hoping you would say that, because I really need to speak with Billy's mother while you children are having some much needed fun, and of course Billy is to come back here with us for tea isn't he?'

'If that is still alright Mrs Agnes? We really don't want to put you to any trouble.'

'It is no trouble at all; now which way should we go? The woods are so pretty this time of year with all the bluebells out.'

Seeing how quiet and subdued Ann is, I decide to try and encourage her to say something.

'I think Ann should decide which way we are going today, so which will it be?'

Ann just looks at me, her eyes red from crying, and her cheeks still stained with her many tears.

'Do I have to come mama? I think I would rather visit the secret place alone today.'

'Ann darling, I know how desperate you are feeling, but that is why we must stay together today, besides you will not be able to spend time with Elizabeth and Eva after tomorrow. We are all going to have to be strong now, you know that don't you? Now, Elizabeth has asked you a question, so it would be impolite not to answer her wouldn't it?'

'The woods are quiet; can we go that way please?'
Both Eva and I were secretly hoping she would say that, but are still very concerned for our friend. This is so unlike her, but how can we help if we don't know what has happened?

'Now that is decided, Ann, you go up and splash your face, the girls and I will wait for you in the garden.'
Ann makes her way upstairs as we follow her mother out into the garden. We seem to be waiting for ages, but just as her mother is about to go in and collect her, Ann joins us once more. She is still very solemn and quiet, but at least she is with us.

The woods are indeed lovely with a carpet of bluebells in every direction, but after seeing Ann's secret place yesterday, nowhere else will ever seem more beautiful to us. Even this morning when we close our eyes, we can still see and feel its peace and sense of calm.

We arrive at the farm just before lunch, so are all invited to join Billy and the rest of his family at the table. After such a pretty walk Eva and I accept eagerly. Ann and her mother also accept the invitation, although Ann barely eats anything. Even Billy seems unable to make Ann smile, despite being told off by his mother several times for his antics at the table. All the time we are eating, I can tell by the expression on Billy's mother's face that she knows something is wrong and, that is the reason for our presence here today.

'Well, this is an unexpected pleasure, is there a special reason for your visit today, or is it just a social call?'

'I'm afraid there are two reasons Joan, and I fear neither of them will meet with enthusiasm.'

'Why my dear Agnes, what is troubling you so? I could sense when you came in that none of you are your usual selves.'
Joan addresses all of us in turn, looking at each of us with obvious concern.

'Well, I think perhaps Eva and Elizabeth should share their news first, and then I must speak with you alone please?'

'Why of course Agnes. Well my dears, what have you got to tell us?'
Both Eva and I have been dreading this moment since we got here, telling Billy was never going to be easy, but we were hoping to

wait until we were back at Ann's for tea. Now, as we look across the table at him, we fear he may already have guessed. Will he even want to come back now?

'Come along girls, you have certainly got a question you wish to ask young Billy do you not?'
Ann's mother's gentle, but firm encouragement leaves us with very little choice. Eva is the first to summon up enough courage.

'We are going away on Monday, and would really like Billy to come back with us for tea today please?'

'Well this is all very sudden I must say. Why the sudden rush? If you don't mind me asking?'

'What Eva is trying to say is that we are going to be returning to live with our mother, although not in London. She has moved up to the north, and we are joining her there. She is so lonely and sad since father has been missing, and she needs us to help her.'

'I knew where you were going already, because you have invited Billy for a visit if you remember, but why so soon?'

'I'm afraid that is my fault, and part of what I need to say to you this afternoon, but Billy is indeed invited to join us for a farewell tea party when we return home later. That is of course with your permission?'

'Can I ma? Please say I can, I don't want Eva and Elizabeth to go away, but now they are, I must at least be allowed to say goodbye to them. Please say you will let me go back for tea with them ma?'

'Oh very well Billy, but you must not cause your Aunt any problems with your silliness, or you will be in big trouble when you get home here, is that clear?'

'Yes ma, I promise to be good, and thank you so much for asking me Aunt Agnes.'

'You are more than welcome Billy. Now perhaps you could take the girls outside for a while so I can speak with your mother, can you do that for me?'

'Course I can, I've got so much I can show them, and this will be my last chance. Come on, let's go!'

'Mama, can I not stay here with you today? I don't really want to go outside again.'

'Now Ann, you know I said to you this morning, don't you?'

Ann nods, and reluctantly agrees to come with us, but only after her mother has said she can return after half an hour if she really needs too.

Once we are outside again, even Ann seems to brighten up a little, and the afternoon speeds by far too quickly. Before we know it we are back at the farmhouse, saying our final farewells to Billy's family. This is really hard, but the journey back to Ann's with Billy is certainly not dull or sad. He knows so much about plants and animals that he keeps dashing off in all directions determined that we shouldn't miss a single thing. By now even Ann seems to be enjoying herself again.

The tea party is so lovely, that Eva and I feel thoroughly spoiled and almost guilty for having such fun when there seems to be such sadness in the house. But, even Tom comes down from his room to join in. At least we know he is alright.'

'I owe you two girls so much, and I could never let you go without saying a proper farewell. I will never forget what you did for me, or what you have brought to this family, so thank you. I know your mother will be greatly comforted and blessed by your presence during such a difficult time for you all.'

Now it is Eva and I who are crying.

'You have all been so kind, we are going to miss you all terribly.'

'Eva is right, we cannot even begin to thank you enough for all you have done, but we will never forget you all either.'

'Now, now girls, this is supposed to be a party, not a time for tears. I fear we may all be shedding enough of those in the days and weeks to come, without starting now. Dry your eyes, then take Billy out into the garden for a few minutes before he has to go home.'

Out in the garden, Billy actually seems lost for words.

'Can you not think of anything to say Billy? You are not usually this quiet.'

'I know, but I never knew you had a garden like this Ann, I'd be out here all the time if I lived here.'

Eva and I just glance at each other, before turning to look at Ann, but she seems to have read our thoughts, and is already heading towards the secret place.

'Are we playing hide and seek?'

'No Billy, but if you promise not to tell anyone, I think Ann wants to show you something very special, is that right Ann?'

'Yes, but you must promise to keep this a secret. I know how excited you can get, and then you might say something to someone about it and that must not happen. No-one else can ever know, do you promise not to tell?'

'You sounded just like my ma then Ann, but I do promise. I don't mean to say things, but sometimes they just come out.'

'This must never come out Billy, please say you will keep our secret?'

'I will, I promise.'

Ann, Eva and I all slip behind the creeper and out of Billy's sight.

'Hey, where are you?'

'Shh! We are here, behind the creeper.'
We have all stopped before we even enter the garden, a fox and her cubs are playing in the far corner. Billy is now beside us, and we are able to stand and watch them for several minutes before the mother fox sees us and quickly leads her cubs back into hiding and safety.

'I have never seen them here before, they are so sweet, I must tell mother when we get back, I'm sure she has never seen them or she would have told me.'

We do not intend to spend long in the secret place, but something seems to be holding us there. It is only when the sun begins to disappear completely from view and the chill in the evening air causes us to shiver, we realise how long we have been here.

'What time do you have to be home tonight Billy?'

'Why? Don't you want me here anymore? I thought we were having fun together?'

'Oh Billy, Elizabeth doesn't mean she wants you to go, it is just that we both suddenly remembered your mother saying something about you being home before it got dark, and looking at the sky, I think we have been out here too long.'

'I think they are right Billy, and besides it is getting cold out here now anyway.'
Ann begins to make her way back to the creeper-covered wall. We follow on assuming Billy is behind us, but as we start to make our way back through to the main garden, Eva turns round and notices Billy standing motionless exactly where we left him.

'Billy, come on, you won't be able to see the way back when it does get dark.'

'Shh! Listen!'

'What, what is it now?'
The three of us stop half in and half out of the creeper trying to hear whatever it is that Billy has obviously just heard.

'Can you hear it?'

'Hear what? I can't hear any…'
A haunting, echoing hoot stops Eva immediately mid-sentence.

'What was that? Is it… is it a ghost?'
Ann's face has gone almost white with fear, and looking at Eva, I think we are all feeling the same.

Billy finally begins to move slowly and quietly towards us, but he appears to be trying not to laugh.

'That's no ghost, that noise we all just heard is the sound of a tawny owl. You girls should see yourselves; owls won't do us no harm.'

In spite of his obvious amusement, Billy's voice is little more than a whisper.

'Well, where is it then?'

Just then a large dappled-brown bird, with the biggest round eyes we have ever seen, swoops down over our heads and lands above us on the only part of the wall that is showing through the creeper. It does not stay perched up there for long, and very soon disappears once more into the ever increasingly-darkening sky.

'Come on, we really must go, mother will be worried if we are out here after dark.'

This time we all slip back through the creeper and emerge into the main garden just in time, because Ann's mother is already at the door, and behind her we can just make out Billy's father.

'Pa, what are you doing here? I'd told ma I'd be alright on my own.'

'Your ma and I don't want you out alone after dark young Billy, you know that, not with this war on and the blackouts being enforced so rigidly right now.'

'Can we go back through the woods pa? I love going that way in the dark.'

'Only if you come away right now, or we will never get home tonight. Now say your goodbyes, I'll wait for you out here by the gate.'

With that Billy's father leaves the four of us in the dimly lit doorway of Ann's house.

'Ann, can you come in here a moment please? Leave the girls and Billy to say their farewells alone. You will get your chance on Monday.'

'But mama.'

'Now Ann please, do not argue with me darling, tonight I need your support, not your disobedience.'

Reluctantly, and with a great deal of sighing, Ann went into the sitting room to join her mother.

'Well I suppose this is it then, this is goodbye. Promise me you will take care of yourselves and your ma when you get there won't you?'

'Come on Billy; don't take all night my boy.'

Billy's father has been very patient, but mild frustration can even be heard the voice of this usually quiet mild-mannered man.

'You better hurry Billy; don't go getting into trouble because of us. Oh Billy, we are going to miss you so much, please say you will write to us?'

'And visit when we are settled?'

'I will Eva, I promise. I'm not that good at letter writing Lizzie, but I will try.'

The three of us stand embracing each other for several minutes, never wanting to let each other go. However, daylight has all but gone and Billy's father has been very understanding up until now, but as I glance over Billy's shoulder, even I can see this patience and understanding is running low.

'Billy, you must go now, the longer you stay here, the harder it will be for all of us. Thank you for being such a friend and for calling me Lizzie, no-one has done that apart from Eva, since we left London.'

'That's alright, you know where I am, and I'll always be your friend.'

Eva and I watch as Billy and his father fade into the ever-darkening woods, before closing the door and making our way to the sitting room, where we join Ann and her mother.

We get up early this morning, after a very restless and sleepless night, putting on our Sunday best ready to attend church as usual. The sun is shining intensely this morning, and the walk home after the service should fill us with warmth and hope, instead the reality of tomorrow is casting a heavy cloud over us. The news of Ann's father being sent to fight in Africa is obviously casting the same sort of cloud over Ann and her mother.

There is none of the usual chatter, and somehow the journey seems to be over all too soon. When we arrive back at the house, Eva and I return to our room to take off our best clothes, ready to pack them and put on our somewhat faded, but prettiest normal dresses before going down for lunch, not that any of us feel much like eating. However, when we get down to the kitchen, Ann and her mother are waiting for us.

'You need not have taken your best clothes off today girls; Ann has something for each of you.'

'I want you to have these, so that you never forget me.'
She now reveals two of the prettiest little hats we have ever seen.

'Oh Ann, we cannot take these, what will your father say? They really are too precious, and we could never forget you anyway.'

'Please take them, I know how much you have admired them, and I want you to have them. Papa is not here, and besides, they are not his, they are mine.'
For the first time in two days, we see a glimpse of the old Ann returning.

'Well if it makes you smile again we will take them, but you must take these.'

'Your ribbons! But I can't, I gave them back to you. They should never have been given to me at all.'

'But we want you to have them Ann, we cannot wear hats and ribbons tomorrow now, can we?'

'Thank you, thank you both; I will
166

wear them all in the morning just for you.'

After lunch, we remember all that we had seen in the secret place with Billy last night, and although it brings a lump to our throats, we remind Ann so she can tell her mother. To our surprise, Ann's mother already knew they were there.

'Why do you think I wanted you to go out there last night?'

'But mama, why did you not tell me they were there?'

'Because my darling, some things are better discovered for ourselves.'

That is exactly what our own mother used to say to us. Our reality is finally beginning to bring hope back to us as we realise that very soon, she will be saying it to us again.

We never thought we could be happy here, but now we are and we have to leave. We thought once we would be so glad to see the back of this place where we had not ever been wanted or wanted to be, but so much has changed. Now, although we are desperate to see our mother again, we are going to another new place and are both scared. We are to travel alone, and the journey is going to be long, we also don't know what to expect when we reach our destination. We will be thrilled to see mother, but father will not be there. Our family has been torn apart.

Our aunt and uncle although kind, are

known to be strict about discipline and behaviour. They are also quite rich and live in a large country house set in huge gardens which we know will be great fun to explore. But still we don't want to leave. As we arrive at the station, tears are flowing freely. Even Ann's mother's eyelashes are twinkling with moisture in spite of her trying to smile. With our goodbyes said, and final hugs done, Eva and I board the train, taking a seat near the window so we can keep Ann and her mother in our sight for as long as possible.

Part
5

We all miss father so very much, and mother can often be heard crying, we just wish there could be some definite news of what has happened to him. Unfortunately, we have been told so often lately that the answers we want may never come, as many have been lost and not yet found. The war has changed everything and laughter just does not come as easily anymore. Our house was always full of laughter and joy, now we just seem to go from day to day with no real pleasure at all. Eva and I feel so guilty and often blame ourselves for going away; regularly telling ourselves that if we had stayed with mother in London, everything might be turning out so differently.

All our friends have gone back to London and we miss them so much, especially when we are at school. We also miss the well-known streets and smells of London, and the friendly people with their familiar accents. Our new school has been even worse than we feared, all the children have their own groups of friends and we are treated like unwelcome intruders all over again. Most of the time they hardly even seem to notice us, and the teacher tries to be kind, but she is really hard to understand. Her northern accent sounds so strange to us, even more strange than Billy's had been. Oh how we miss Ann and Billy. Life with Ann and her parents may have been really bad for us to begin with, but when we left, it was like saying goodbye to our own mother all over again. Only this time, we felt like we were leaving our sister as well.

Both Eva and I are struggling a lot, and it is taking ages to even begin to settle in at all. The house is nice though, it is thatched (this is what the straw on the roof is called), but can it ever really be home? At least we were able to move into our new home straight away when we arrived. Having our cousins living close by helps a bit, and today Eliza has been telling us about a maze which is hidden behind the small wood. This wood can be seen from the windows at the back of our cottage, but the maze cannot be seen until you get into the middle of the woods. Eliza has even promised to take us, so the next time she comes over we have decided to make straight for there. Life is hard and everything is still being rationed. We just cannot believe that we can ever be truly happy again.

***

Spring is now turning into summer, and this morning we have received a letter from Ann. We write to her and Billy regularly,

Ann always writes straight back, but we are still waiting to get any letters from Billy. The letter which has arrived this morning is especially important because we are hoping it will be the answer to our invitation for her to visit us up here this summer. We don't know it has arrived until we get home from school, but now we cannot wait to open it and read everything it says. However, any excitement and hope that had started to build inside us, soon disappears completely. Ann isn't going to come after all. She says that her mother does not want her to be away for that long at the moment and that she would feel guilty about leaving her mother with her father so far away.

'Do you think she will ever come and see us Lizzie?'
Eva's voice clearly displaying the intense disappointment we are both now feeling.

'I don't know Eva, but I do wish Billy would write back just once. I hate it here; I want to go back to London.'
Eva looks startled at my sudden outburst, but I know that she is feeling the same.

We have been to the maze several times with Cousin Eliza, but now even going there seems pointless. We so much want to show it, and the stream beyond to Ann and Billy, but are beginning to doubt whether we will ever get the chance. At least there is only one more

172

horrible week of school left before the holidays, but then we will have even less to do.

There is still no more news about father, and the thought of the long hot summer days without him, is almost overbearing for all three of us. Nothing will ever be the same again. We should be looking forward to carefree days in the sun, picnics in meadows and trips to the seaside. Although our dear mother has said she will try and do some of these things with us, we know it will never feel the same without father.

Our cousins Eliza and Cyril are alright, but they are both older than us, and seem to either want to tell us what to do, or else they can't be bothered with us at all. Eliza is not quite as bad as Cyril, but we just keep feeling in the way when we are with them. Mother is busy some of the time now too; she is a volunteer with the Woman's Royal Voluntary Service, or WRVS for short. She seems to enjoy being with the other ladies, and even seems happier when she comes home, at least for a while. Eva and I don't mind her doing this; it is just that we feel so lonely and alone up here. But, today mother has come home and told us about a new girl in the village, she wants us to go and see her to try and make her feel welcome.

'How can we make her feel welcome if

173

we don't even feel welcome here ourselves?'

'Oh Eva, I was hoping that you and your sister would have at least started to settle in by now. Please my darlings, can you try and be happy here? I know how much you miss London and your father, I do too. I also know how disappointed you are that Ann is unable to come, but we have to try and make a life up here now, for the three of us. Making friends with Violet might even help you as much as it helps her; at least you would all have a friend.'

'How do you know it will help her mother?

'I know it will help her Eva because she has no brothers or sisters, she is living with her aunt and uncle since her parents were both killed when a bomb hit their house in Liverpool.'

'You mean she is all alone up here? Hasn't she got any cousins?'

'No my darling, her aunt and uncle have no children of their own, so were only too glad to offer Violet a home with them. Don't forget, she has been through a lot, so you will need to be patient and give her some time. But at least she will know someone when school starts again. She only lives five minutes away, and I told her aunt that you would be round this afternoon so off you pop while I get the washing in off the line, and start getting tea ready.'

'Do we have to go now?'

'Lizzie, please try and make some effort, you are usually the one I can rely on to rise to a new challenge. I know life is hard at the moment for all of us, but at least we still have each other. Violet has nobody, and from what her aunt has been telling me she has always been shy, but now she barely speaks at all. I thought that perhaps meeting people of her own age might help a little. Why don't you and Eva go and show her the maze?'

Reluctantly, Eva and I make our way to the cottage next to the post office where Violet is now living, and timidly knock on the little door. We have often thought how pretty this little house is, with its little porch covered in roses, but never dreamed we would have any reason to visit.

While we are waiting in the hot summer sun for the door to be opened, a strangely familiar scent seems to almost transport us back to place deep in our memory, but before we can place it the door opens, and a cheery, round little lady introduces herself. Although, not before guessing who we are.

'You must be Elizabeth and Eva; I am Maud, Violet's aunt, thank you so much for coming. Violet is in the garden at the back, would you like to join her there?'

'Thank you that would be lovely.'

Eva and I follow Maud through the little cottage, out into the prettiest little garden we have seen since we arrived here. Ours is going to be nice, but it needs a lot of looking after to get it to look like mother wants it too.

'Now, how about some homemade elderflower cordial girls? You must be thirsty with this heat. Violet, this is Elizabeth and Eva; they have come to see you. They are new here too, so you all need a friend right now.'

Violet is small for her age, with ginger hair and freckles. She looks up and tries to smile, but her pain is all too clear for us to see.

'Thank you for coming, I'm afraid that I am not very good company at the moment.'

'I'm afraid that we are not very good company either. We have been here about six weeks now, but we still feel as if we don't belong here. When we left London, we were sent to stay with strangers, but we did not want to leave them to come here. We miss Ann and Billy so much, and nobody here wants to make friends.'

'Well maybe at least the three of us can be friends? Do you think we can Violet?'

'I would really like to have somebody else to talk too. Aunty Maud and Uncle Jack are lovely, and so kind, but I miss all my friends in Liverpool too.'

We find that in spite of ourselves, we have

a really nice time with Violet, and for the first time since we came here, we begin to feel hope again. As we leave Violet and begin our short walk home, the scent we smelt outside the cottage is still trying to take us back to somewhere else. But, by the time we get home that too is just a memory.

'Did you girls have a nice time? Tea is ready, and you can tell me about your afternoon while we eat.'

'Thank you mother, we are so sorry that we have been so awful since we came here. It is just that we have been forced to move from London to live with strangers, and when we had finally settled in, we have had to move again and come here. This war is horrid, and we just want it to be over!'

'I am so sorry my darlings, I know this has been hard for you, but you both seem happier this evening. Why don't you tell me about Violet?'

We spend the rest of the evening talking to mother about Violet, and the plans we have made with her for the rest of the summer. We go to bed tonight still missing Ann and Billy, but with a new found friend who feels as lost and lonely as we do. Finally, things slowly seem to be getting more bearable for us.

We visit Violet everyday over the next few weeks, and every time the scent near the front of the cottage keeps trying to take us back to a different time and place. It is only as we arrive today, and the scent is absent, that we remember where we have smelt it before. It was in the secret place in Ann's garden. Oh how we both long to be able to take Violet there. She would love it as much as we did, and we know that she and Ann would be such good friends. It is only now that we realise Ann has not replied to our last two letters. Maybe she has forgotten about us after all? Billy still hasn't written back either, but he did tell us before we left that letters weren't his thing, so maybe we should stop sending them? As we are thinking about all these things, Maud opens the door, and once again provides us with a glass of her homemade elderflower cordial which is delicious. As usual the afternoon is spent at the maze and by the stream, before returning to Violet's house for another glass of cordial before Eva and I go home.

Before leaving today, we ask Maud what the scent near the front door had been, and she tells us that it is called lavender. When we ask why we had not smelt it today, she explains that she has cut it and hung it up to dry before the winter gets here.

'Why? What do you do with it then?' We know we should not ask so many questions, but it seems a strange thing to do with flowers.

'Well, I make up little lacy bags, fill them with the lavender and then they can be put between your clothes in a cupboard or a chest of drawers to make them smell nice. You can have one each when they are ready if you like? But that won't be for a while yet.'
Still feeling a little unsure and confused about what we have just been told, we thank Maud for her kindness, and make our way home. As we do so, we are very aware that this summer has been much better than we thought it would be, and at least when we return to school next week, we will have one new friend and Violet will have two.

***

Now we are back at school, every day is almost the same. Having Violet as a friend is certainly helping us to adjust to life up here, but still none of the other children seem to want to get to know us at all. We are finally beginning to understand our teacher a bit better now; we both think that getting to know Violet has helped that too. Her accent is not quite the same, but we got used to hers over the summer, so when the teacher says something now it seems clearer than it was before.

The weather up here seems really strange; the seasons appear to change so quickly. The leaves on the trees are already glowing in all their autumn colours, and there is already a chill in the air. Nothing up here is the same as in London, or even down where Ann lives. It is only just October and there has already been snow on the tops of the mountains only a few miles away. Mum has already been warned by Violet's Aunt Maud to get in enough provisions to last a few months, as getting anywhere to buy more when winter sets in is going to be close to impossible.

'But how are we supposed to get extra provisions when everything is still being rationed?'

'You don't need extra dearie; you just need to use what you have differently. Just make sure you use you fresh food first and keep as many tins and packets as you can. All you really need to do is get your full allowance of everything you are entitled too. You might be able to get out for fresh goods once a week if you are lucky but sometimes even that isn't possible.'

'What do you mean, will nowhere be open?'

'More like you won't be able to get there if they are. I am not trying to frighten or alarm you, but when the bad weather sets in, we sometimes can't even get to our own front gate the snow is that deep.'

Mother is not used to thick snow coming from London, even in bad weather you can still get about. We saw thick snow last year at Ann's, but we still went out, but Maud makes it sound as though winter could be tougher than we thought. Mother is already starting to heed Maud's warning, and taking her advice, we now get pie or stew every day with fresh meat.

This morning when we get up it is so cold that there is frost on the inside of the window in our bedroom, so we waste no time in getting dressed and going downstairs. It is not much warmer down here, but at least mother has got the range on and the porridge for breakfast is already cooked. Although we usually complain about porridge every day, saying we are fed up with it, the warm sticky mixture is almost soothing this morning.

'Make sure you wrap up warm today girls, winter seems to have got here already.'
As soon as we leave our cottage to walk to school, collecting Violet on our way as usual, we can really feel the difference.

'I hope it is not going to get any colder Lizzie, I don't think I will be able to go out at all.'

'I know Eva, last year was cold but I fear winter will be worse up here.'
Violet is wrapped up too, but the cold still seems to get through. So much so that our face, hands and feet are really hurting before we even get to school. By the time we get home, we are so tired and we are aching all

181

over from the cold, we don't even notice the letter addressed to us on the table.

'Why is it so cold mother? It makes everything hurt!'

'I know my darlings, come in and sit by the fire, tea is almost ready.'

Glancing at the table she continues.

'You haven't opened your letter yet, I think it must be from your friend Ann, although the writing seems different.'

'A letter for us mother, where is it?'

'I put it on the table so that you would see it when you came in.'

Eva gets there first and has it opened before I can even see the envelope.

'It isn't from Ann Lizzie; it is from Billy, at last. He says he couldn't write before, because has been too busy helping his father on the farm. But now winter has arrived, there is less he can do, so he has written to us before we forget him.'

'I can read it for myself Eva.'

'I'm sorry Lizzie, it is just that I did not expect it to be from Billy and I was excited.'

'I feel the same Eva, but how could we ever forget Billy? I wonder why Ann hasn't written since the letter saying she was unable to come and see us.'

'Do you think she is alright Lizzie?'

'I don't know Eva, but I really do hope so. Her mother should have had the baby by now.'

'I'm sure she will write again when she can my darlings. Now, up to the table, tea is ready and must be eaten while it's hot.'

We are soon proved right. We thought that last winter was bad, but the winter up here is so bitterly cold with really heavy snow, the likes of which none of us have seen before and which can only be described as cruel. With Christmas coming, mother has promised that we will celebrate it, even with the struggles this war brings with it. So, we are both trying to be happy and look forward to it. Nothing feels the same anymore, and preparing for Christmas with such a significant member of our family missing is so hard.

It is Christmas Eve, our first Christmas since we moved up here and since our father has been missing. We really are happy to be back with mother, but we still feel like strangers up here in the north. We are all missing father terribly, and because there has never been any further news, we are still finding hard to believe he has really gone. But tonight as we are getting into bed, our mother's face is different; there is what appears to be a twinkle in her eyes that has been missing for a long time. She seems almost as happy, as she used to be before the war started.

'Are you happier than when we first came here mother? Eva and I don't really mind living here as long as we can spend Christmas with just you, and presents don't matter either.'

With her face shining, and tears glistening in her eyes, our mother bends down to kiss us goodnight, whispering gently to us as she does so.

'Not all presents come in boxes that are wrapped in pretty paper my darlings.'

'What do you mean mother?'

'It's a surprise Eva, you will see when tomorrow comes, but unless you and your sister both go to sleep now, you will be too tired in the morning to enjoy yourselves.'

'Thank you mother, we love you.'

'That's alright my sweethearts, I love you too. Now goodnight, sleep well, and no sneaking downstairs!'

'We promise.'

'You are my good girls; I know you won't let me down.'

The door closes and mother makes her way back downstairs. As we lay there we keep thinking about what mother has just said about presents and cannot help wondering what she could possibly mean. This is our final thought as we fall asleep.

When we wake up this morning, mother can be heard downstairs, already busy in the kitchen, so both Eva and I grab our dressing gowns and run downstairs. Breakfast is ready so Eva and I both sit down and after wishing our mother a Happy Christmas, we begin to eat. It is only now that we realise that there are four places set at the table. But before we can ask why, our mother asks us to close our eyes. Eva and I look at each other curiously, we think this a strange request, but do it without question, and after only a few seconds we can hear the door opening behind us.

'Hello my darlings.'

This strangely familiar voice brings a lump into my throat, and Eva cannot disguise her shock as she gasps in surprise.

'Happy Christmas.'

We both know immediately who it is. Forgetting that I am now twelve years old, I find myself saying something I never thought I would say again.

'Daddy! Is it really you?'

I am crying and tears are streaming down my face as I sob this out.

'It is.'

This reply, in his own, dear gentle voice is more than I could ever have hoped for.

'Oh my own dearest father, I knew you would never leave us without saying goodbye. I always said you would come home one day.'

'Oh Eva, I will never not believe you again.'
We are both now hugging him as tightly as we can, and he has wrapped us in his strong arms like he always used to. We are determined that we are never letting him go again. This is certainly going to be our best Christmas ever.

Dear Reader
If you have enjoyed reading this book, then
please leave a review on Amazon.
Thank you.

About the Author

Elizabeth Manning-Ives is the pen name of published poet Helen Thwaites and 'When Tomorrow Comes' is her third novel. Her first two books 'Living Under the Shadow' and 'A Journey of Significance' have both received 5 star reviews on Amazon. As well as writing, Helen also enjoys a variety of handicrafts, nature and playing the flute. In the past she has also been involved with many amateur dramatics productions locally. She is heavily involved with her church where she currently enjoys the challenge of helping with a service at a local residential care home once a month. She loves chocolate and insists that it stimulates and enhances her writing.

To find out more about Elizabeth or to follow her on social media visit
https://emiauthor76.wordpress.com/